C0-BPD-192

Ernestine & Amanda

Mysteries on Monroe Street

Ernestine & Amanda

MYSTERIES ON

Monroe Street

❧ *Sandra Belton* ☙

SIMON & SCHUSTER BOOKS FOR YOUNG READERS

ATHENS REGIONAL LIBRARY
2025 BAXTER STREET
ATHENS, GA 30606

SIMON & SCHUSTER BOOKS FOR YOUNG READERS
An imprint of Simon & Schuster Children's Publishing Division
1230 Avenue of the Americas, New York, New York 10020

Copyright © 1998 by Sandra Belton
All rights reserved including the right of reproduction in whole or in part in any form.
SIMON & SCHUSTER BOOKS FOR YOUNG READERS is a trademark of Simon & Schuster.
Book design by Heather Wood • The text for this book is set in Goudy Old Style.
Printed and bound in the United States of America
10 9 8 7 6 5 4 3 2 1 First Edition

Library of Congress Cataloging-in-Publication Data
Belton, Sandra.
Ernestine & Amanda, mysteries on Monroe Street / Sandra Belton.
p. cm. — (Ernestine & Amanda)
Summary: Ernestine and Amanda, two African-American twelve-year-olds growing up
under segregation in the 1950s, are brought together when the all-black dance studio
where they take lessons is attacked by vandals. ISBN 0-689-81612-X
[1. Dance—Fiction. 2. Race relations—Fiction. 3. Afro Americans—Fiction.
4. Friendship—Fiction.] I. Title. II. Series: Belton, Sandra. Ernestine & Amanda.
PZ7.B4197Et 1998 [Fic]—dc21 97-45013 CIP AC

For Miriam Hughes Raymond,
a pure joy of a friend!

Ernestine & Amanda

Mysteries on Monroe Street

Ernestine & Amanda

"HEY, ERNESTINE! Wait up!"

"Oh, hi, Amanda. I didn't see you."

"I guess not. You were so busy listenin' to Wilhelmina. What was she tellin' you, anyhow? Did you find out anything new?"

"Whadda you mean? New about what?"

"About Monroe Street, Ernestine. You know, everything that's been happening down here. What else would I be talkin' about?"

"How would I know? I can't read your mind."

"Nobody's askin' you to, Ernestine. All I asked was did Wilhelmina tell you anything about what's been happenin' down here on Monroe Street."

"That's not what you asked me, Amanda. You said—"

"Ernestine, I *know* what I said. *You* know what I meant."

"You oughta say what you mean, Amanda, then I wouldn't have to try to read your mind."

"What's all this 'read your mind' mess? How come you can't just answer my question?"

"Maybe 'cause you didn't *ask* your question. What you asked was—"

"Forget it, Ernestine! Just forget it!"

"Forget what? You haven't said anything for me to forget, Amanda!"

"You know somethin', Ernestine, what I think is—"

"I *know* plenty, Amanda, but like I said, since I can't read your mind, one thing I *don't* know is what you think."

"Well, here's one thing you *can* know, Ernestine Harris. All I was doin' in the first place was askin' you a simple question. And I asked it nice! You're the one who started makin' somethin' out of it."

"I'm not makin' nothin' out of anything! How come you always accusing me of junk?"

"All I asked was did you hear anything new about what's been happening on Monroe Street. That's *all* I said."

"Amanda, that's *not* what you said. If you had said that, I woulda known how to answer instead of havin' to ask you what you were talkin' about."

"Ernestine, why do you always make it so hard to talk to you?"

"*I'm* not the one who makes it hard, Amanda. It's you!"

"It is *not* me! All I said was—"

"Are we gonna go over that *again*? Look, Amanda—"

"No, *you* look, Ernestine. And you need to *listen*, too...."

1 ☙ Ernestine

SEEMS LIKE THE MORE *things keep changin', the more they keep stayin' the same.*

Grandmother Carroll's saying kept coming into my head while I walked down Fourth Street. Everywhere I walked I saw things that were changing and not changing at the same time. Like Fourth Street Elementary where I had gone to school from first to fifth grade and where Mama would be teaching when school started.

When I was at Fourth Street, Mama hadn't even gotten her teaching certificate yet, and now she was going to be the second-grade teacher. There was going to be a different third-grade teacher, too, and a new principal. But the school looked like it always has. Same old dirty red brick building and playground without any grass left anywhere. Same rusty sliding board with the dent right in the middle that T-Bone

Carson's crazy brother made one night, trying to wreck things on the playground because he had been suspended from school for a week.

It was strange to see the playground so empty. There weren't even any of the little neighborhood kids on the swings and jungle gym like there usually are.

Probably too hot.

The weather was one of the reasons I had decided to take a walk. I figured walking under all the big trees along Fourth Street would cool me off. But the main reason was wanting to get away from my house and everything else on Second Street that reminded me so much of Clovis and how lonesome it was without him. Every time I looked at his house, which is next door to mine, I would remember that he wouldn't be coming back from Georgia until Christmas. And maybe not even then.

Things had really gotten bad when I saw Clovis's grandmother picking blackberries from the bushes in her yard. "Hey there, Ernestine!" She had waved at me with a hand full of berries.

"Hey, Gramma Taylor," I said. I waved back at her.

"I'm counting on you to help me finish up this blackberry cobbler I'm making," she called. "With Clovis gone it'll just be sitting there."

"Yes, Ma'am," I said, and waved again.

I couldn't say anything else because I could feel my throat closing up and tears coming to my eyes. That's when I jumped up from the porch where I had been sitting, and told Jazz to tell Mama that I was going for a walk.

"What for?" Jazz yelled from the sidewalk where she was drawing pictures with chalk.

"'Cause I want to," I yelled back. Then I ran out of the yard and across the street before she could say anything else to me.

As soon as I got to Fourth Street, I found out I had figured wrong about everything. It wasn't cool at all under the trees. The heat was everywhere. It even came up from the sidewalk and went through my shoes into my feet. And the whole time I walked, I couldn't think about anything *but* Clovis. How the two of us had walked down this same street every day for years. Going to school or back home. How sometimes we used to race each other, betting an ice-cream cone for the winner. When he won, Clovis would always get a chocolate cone from Mr. Cleveland's store.

I hope the chocolate ice cream in Georgia stinks!

I tried shaking my head to get all the thinking about Clovis out. But that didn't work, either. Plus I felt kinda dumb, standing there on the sidewalk by myself, shaking my head. Lucky for me there wasn't anybody around.

I walked over to the school to look into my old fifth-grade classroom. Maybe seeing how the room looked now would give me something different to think about.

When I looked through the window, all I saw was chairs piled up on the desks and bare walls. There wasn't even anything across the top of the blackboard. Like the fancy letter cards Mrs. Lawson would tap her long pointer on while she was telling us how horrendous our handwriting was. But it was still the same classroom we had sat in day after day.

Somethin' else changin' and not changin' at the same time.

It was easy to picture how we had been in that room. Clovis's desk was right behind mine in the third row. Sylvia Parnell sat in front of me and Jackson Moss had sat behind Clovis. Mrs. Lawson didn't make everybody sit in alphabetical order like our fourth-grade teacher had. The only reason Mrs. Lawson made anybody sit someplace special was for talking or cheating or making trouble.

My face was so close to the window, I could smell the classroom. Even though it was August and there hadn't been any school for two months, I still recognized the smells. Chalk dust. Stale bologna sandwiches. Sweaty socks. Smells that had been there forever.

Everything being so much the same and different was making me feel worse.

Maybe I'll walk over to Du Bois. There're probably kids all over that playground.

W.E.B. Du Bois Elementary is where I went for sixth grade. All the Fourth Street Elementary kids have to go there. Fourth Street only goes to fifth, but Du Bois goes all the way to eighth. After that, everybody goes to Banneker High School.

At first it was horrible being at Du Bois. The school is a lot bigger than Fourth Street, and I figured that would make it a lot harder. But everything turned out okay. I even entered the W.E.B. Du Bois Festival they have every year. The oratorical contest part.

Another good thing about Du Bois was being in the same school with Alicia Raymond. She's been at Du Bois since first grade, but I haven't known her that long. We met from taking piano lessons together. We don't take lessons on the same day anymore, but we're still good friends. Alicia is almost a best friend.

But nobody can take Clovis's place. Not even Alicia.

I really wanted to stop thinking about Clovis. But it seemed like I just couldn't.

It'll probably get worse if I walk to Du Bois. Then I'll remember how lonesome I'm gonna be practically the whole entire year!

I was at the corner of Fourth and Jackson, waiting for the light to change. Looking up at the Jackson Street sign made me think of Wilhelmina.

Maybe she's back from visiting her parents in North Carolina.

Wilhelmina Washington had been new to Du Bois just like I was. Only she was new to Carey, too. She had lived in New York City before. She had come to Carey to stay with her aunt while her parents moved to North Carolina and found a house for them to live in.

Wilhelmina went to North Carolina to spend the summer with her parents, but she was coming back to stay with her aunt when school started. That's what she told me in the letter she had written from North Carolina.

I had almost fallen over when I got the letter from Wilhelmina. Not because I didn't want to hear from her or anything like that. It's just that she and I aren't really all that close, although she is a friend. She's the one who helped me the most with my speech for the oratorical contest.

Wilhelmina is one of the smartest people I know. She's also one of the most peculiar. Sometimes it feels like I want to be her friend and *don't* want to at the same time. Once when I talked to Mama about how I felt, she started explaining how things in life are never just one color or another but a lot of colors all mixed together. And that people are like that, too.

"*All* people," Mama had said, looking at me. "Including you and me."

It was one of Mama's explanations that kinda caused confusion instead of ending it. I didn't say anything else to Mama about it and decided that one day I'd be able to figure it out.

Thinking about Wilhelmina and her letter made it hit me! I almost wanted to kick myself because I hadn't thought about it sooner.

Ernestine, you're a dummy!

I didn't have to just keep missing Clovis like crazy and feeling awful from seeing things that were changing and not changing at the same time. I could write Clovis a letter. I could write him a *ton* of letters. I could write to him every single day.

And he'll answer every letter. It'll almost be like havin' him here.

I figured I hadn't thought about writing to him before because I hadn't felt much like writing to anybody the whole summer. It wasn't like last summer when I had been at camp. There had been lots to write about at Hilltop. Nothing much happened at Grandmother Carroll's, so I didn't even think about writing letters.

I stopped at the intersection of Fayette and Second Street. If I turned right I would be on my way to Du Bois; if I turned left I would be headed home. I turned left.

After I crossed the street I couldn't keep myself from

remembering how the Second Street corner was one of our favorite starting places for a race home. I could almost hear Clovis and I yelling to each other.

"Last one home is a fool without ice cream," I would say.

"Yeah, 'cause you gonna have to spend your money on ice cream for me," Clovis would yell back. "And I want chocolate!"

"It's Clovis who's gonna be buyin' today," I would say, calling him "CLO-vis," the way he hates to have his name pronounced. He pronounces it "Clo-VEESE."

As hot as it was, I started running. Just like we always had. I knew I would start sweating like crazy, but I didn't care. I had to get home to write my first letter to Clovis. To make myself go faster, I pretended Clovis was right behind me, trying to win that chocolate ice-cream cone.

Grandmother Carroll sure is right: The more things keep changin', the more they keep stayin' the same.

2 ✥ Amanda

"AMANDA! GIRL, you look *good* in that color!"

I tried not to smile when Edna said that, but I couldn't help myself. The color of the leotards and dance skirts *did* look good on me. A lot better than it looked on either Edna *or* Alicia.

When Miss Davis had passed out the dance outfits, I felt like throwing mine in the trash. All of us did. The white leotards she had told us to buy weren't white anymore. They had been dyed a dirty purple color. And if that wasn't bad enough, Miss Davis had made long skirts to match!

"Lookin' at this mess makes me want to puke," Edna had whispered, turning up her nose at her leotards. And Miss Davis had heard her!

"Close, Edna," Miss Davis said.

"Ma'am?" Edna said, trying to look innocent.

"I said, your description of the color is close." Miss Davis was standing in front of Glynice and looking at Edna over her shoulder. "But it's 'puce,' not 'puke.'"

After that, nobody said anything about the outfits. Not even when Miss Davis told us we were supposed to wear them to class *and* to practice in. But as soon as we left the church basement, we had plenty to say. Especially Edna.

"I'm not gettin' up on nobody's stage wearin' this mess," she said while we started walking to my house.

"Who says you have to?" Alicia said, looking at her sister. "Edna, this outfit is for class and to practice in. Nobody said we'll be wearin' it for performances."

Alicia and Edna are twins, but that's hard to believe if no one points it out. In the first place, they don't look anything alike. Alicia looks like their mother, and Edna looks like their father, Dr. Raymond. Edna's okay looking, but Alicia is definitely pretty. That's why I just knew Alicia would look better in the ugly dance stuff than any of us.

Alicia probably thought so, too. "Maybe they'll look okay when we put them on," she said. "Let's go home and try them on."

"It's too hot to try stuff on, especially this pile of puke," Edna said.

"It won't be too hot at my house," I said. "Even upstairs in my room. We have window fans in every room upstairs."

"Okay?" Alicia said, looking at her sister.

Edna looked at the outfit she was carrying and made a face, but she said, "I guess so."

"So, let's go," I said.

For my twelfth birthday, Mother had let me fix up my bedroom like I wanted it. Well, almost. She didn't let me get the bedspread I really wanted, but everything else is just what I picked out. Anyhow, the bedspread we finally got was my second choice.

My best choice was the wallpaper. It looks like clouds, and I finally convinced Mother that instead of covering the walls with it, I should cover the ceiling and only one wall. She and my sister Madelyn said doing it like that would make my bedroom look a mess. They were both wrong. It looks terrific. Putting up the wallpaper like that makes my bedroom look like it's part inside the house and part outside.

Putting up a mirror on the back of my door was Mother's idea. I always had to go to Madelyn's room whenever I wanted to see all of myself. She has a full-length mirror that matches her furniture. Her mirror is prettier than mine, but mine is larger. It covers the entire door.

Besides the fans in the windows, the mirror was one of the reasons I was glad we were going back to my house to try on the dance outfits. Most of the time when we need to do something together, we go to the Raymonds' house. Especially since my dad moved out.

My father left our house to get his own place over a year ago. Mother and Dad said it was just going to be a separation. Sometimes I believe it's more than that. Sometimes I even think they might get a divorce. But when I think that, I know that I'm believing the worst like Madelyn says I do sometimes. I don't think I usually do that, but maybe the thing with my parents is making me.

When Dad first left, it *was* the worst. It was too awful to believe. And I couldn't really talk to anyone about it. It hurt so much for him not to be living at home anymore. I couldn't even talk to Alicia, who's been my best friend for as long as I've had friends. Not even to my Godmother Frankie, who's the best person in the absolute world to talk to about …about things.

Godmother Frankie was the only one who tried to make me talk about the separation. But not trying to be nosy or anything like that. I knew she was doing it to try to make me feel better. Then for my birthday she gave me a diary.

"Your own personal secret keeper, Godchild," Godmother had said after I opened the present and saw what it was. "The name 'Amanda' on it and this little gold key, which there's only one of, make that fact very clear."

Godmother also gave me a gold chain to put the key on. I wear it around my neck every day. I haven't written in the diary yet, though.

I wonder if it's weird to talk to a book?

When Alicia and Edna and I got to my house, Madelyn was in the kitchen making dinner.

"That you, Amanda?" she yelled from the kitchen when she heard the door slam.

"Nope. It's Am-Al-Ed," I yelled back.

"Hello, *Am*-anda, *Al*-icia, *Ed*-na," she said, trying to make my clever joke sound weird.

"Hooray, Madelyn the *unfunny* got it!" I yelled back while the three of us ran up the steps to my room.

When we got our dance things on, the color really didn't seem so bad. And like Edna had said, it didn't look bad at *all* on me.

"I guess I don't hate it as much as I thought I would," I said.

"Well, I hate it more," Edna said.

"It's okay," Alicia said. She started twirling around and around. Her long skirt began to wave in the breeze from the window fan. "And the way the skirt flows out when you turn is nice!"

All three of us got near the fan and started turning in circles like Alicia was doing. We watched ourselves in the mirror.

It is nice the way these skirts curve out.

We twirled around so much and so fast, we started getting dizzy. Finally we fell on the floor, laughing. Nobody minded, though, because my new rug is super soft.

Edna started posing herself on the floor, doing things like stretching her legs out and moving her arms in different positions. She watched herself in the mirror while she moved. "After I get a beautiful dance costume, I'll become a great ballerina," she said. She threw her head back and got an expression on her face like she was *already* famous.

Edna thinks a lot about how things look and being beautiful and famous, and stuff like that. It can really get on your nerves.

Alicia got up and started moving her body into different positions. Only she was *really* trying out dance things. "Miss

Davis made everything about dancin' seem so exciting!" she said. "I can't wait to get started."

"What *I* can't wait to learn is how to leap and turn in the air," Edna said. She started trying to push herself up from the floor and do a leap at the same time. "You know, like Miss Davis did when we had that first meeting."

"You better watch yourself, girl," I said. Edna looked ready to fall on her face.

"Miss Davis is a wonderful dancer," Alicia said, trying out a leap herself. "Don't you think so, Amanda?"

"I guess," I said.

I didn't see how any of us could say much about the teacher's dancing. The first day we met with her to hear about the classes, she had danced a little bit, but not much. Glynice said she was just doing enough to impress everybody.

Edna finally stopped her weird leaping. "You know what I heard about Miss Davis?" Edna said.

"What?" I asked her.

Alicia cut in. "Edna, Mommy keeps tellin' you about that."

"About what?" Edna said.

"About carrying gossip," Alicia said, rolling her eyes at Edna.

"So, how is sayin' that somebody used to dance with Katherine Dunham carrying gossip?" Edna said, rolling her eyes back at Alicia.

"Who?" I asked Edna.

"Oh, yeah," Alicia said before Edna could answer. "That's really true."

"*What's* true?" I said.

"If Alicia would shut up, I could tell you," Edna said, making a face at Alicia.

Alicia rolled her eyes at Edna again, but she didn't say anything.

"What's true," Edna said, "is that Lona Davis, our dance teacher, used to dance with Katherine Dunham. She's even been in the movies!" Edna started posing herself again while she talked.

"Miss Davis was in the *movies?*" I couldn't believe it.

Both Edna and Alicia laughed. Especially Edna. She carried on like I had said something super stupid. I ignored her.

"Katherine Dunham is the one who's been in the movies," Alicia said. "Mommy saw her in *Stormy Weather.*"

Sometimes hearing Alicia and Edna call their mother "Mommy" really gets on my nerves. Especially as old as they are. This was one of those times.

"Well," I said, "it doesn't matter *who* she danced with. The only thing that matters is this: Is she good enough to deal with *me?*"

Right after I said that, I jumped up and did a couple of leaps and twirls around the room. It felt like I was doing it good, and when I saw the look on Edna's face I *knew* that I had been. But Alicia was the one who said so.

"Wow, Amanda," she said, "you're already a good dancer! You *really* are. Isn't she, Edna?"

Edna didn't say anything, she only nodded her head. A sort of half nod. But I didn't care. The look was still on her face.

I didn't say anything about how I had been practicing dance moves for months. Ever since I knew we were going to start having dance classes. I just smiled at Alicia and Edna. Then I looked at myself in my new long mirror.

Ever since the mirror's been up, it's been impossible to keep from staring at myself and noticing absolutely everything. Like how much my legs and even my neck seem to be growing. But standing there with Alicia and Edna and seeing all three of us together in the mirror, I didn't mind my long legs or my neck. In fact, I was glad they were like they are.

And Alicia's right. I look like I'm already a dancer.

I bit on the insides of my cheeks to keep from smiling and looking conceited. And to keep Edna from guessing what I was thinking.

Who knows...maybe someday I'll be the one dancin' with Katherine Dunham!

"Let's go show Madelyn our outfits!" I said, twirling around to open my bedroom door.

3 🐾 Ernestine

August 6, 1957

Dear Clovis,

   I got your letter yesterday! It was great for you to write
back so fast!! And the only reason I waited until today to
write my next letter to you was because of the weather. It
was so hot yesterday I couldn't even think!!!!!

   I hope you won't get mad at me for telling you this, but
I'm a little glad you hate being in Georgia. But not because
I want you to feel depressed like you said you were getting.
It's because I hate you being there, too. It's HORRIBLE
not having you here, and it's going to be worse when school
starts. I might even have to take notes to help me remember all the things you'll have to know about.

   You didn't say anything about school in your letter. Have

you seen where you'll be going? You didn't say anything about anybody you've met, either. Have you met any of the kids who'll be in your class? Actually, Clovis, you didn't give a lot of news, except about how awful it is to be there and how much your dad is bugging you. In your next letter please let me know what's going on.

DARN!!! Mama's yelling at me to come outside on the porch. You know something, lately that's all she does. Yell at me to do stuff. I'm beginning to wish she would just write me notes so I wouldn't have to listen to her so much. But I'll finish telling you about that later. I'd better go and see what she wants before she sends Jazz in to get me and I REALLY get mad!!!!!

   I'll be back in a little while.

As soon as Mama finished talking, she picked up her glass of iced tea and took a drink. I didn't think she could see me looking at her through the glass, so I glared as hard as I could.

"But, how come she wants *me*?" I said.

"Because you're the best, baby. I thought you knew that."

Mama fished in her glass for an ice cube. "Whew!" she said, rubbing the ice along her face and neck. "This August heat is about to do me in."

And you're about to do me *in!*

I had stopped glaring, but I was still looking at Mama. I watched her take another big swallow of tea.

"The dance teacher doesn't even know me," I said.

"But she knows *of* you," Mama said. "Miss Helen made sure of that."

"What's Miss Helen got to do with it?"

The words had flown out of my mouth, sounding just like I was feeling: angry.

Mama turned her head and looked at me. Her ice cube had almost melted away, but she was still moving the little piece up and down her neck.

"Excuse me?" Mama said.

Mama's "cuse" part of "excuse" went up and down and sounded like it was spelled with forty "u's." Even as angry as I was, I knew saying it like that meant only one thing: I was the one who should be thinking about saying "Excuse me."

"I only meant that…uh, I mean, ah, how come Miss Helen would be involved with the dance lady?"

For a while Mama kept looking at me without saying anything. Then she reached into her glass again for another ice cube. There was only one left.

"The young lady who'll be playing regularly for the dance classes is Miss Helen's niece," she said, rolling the cube around in her hand. "Her name is Katy Ferguson. Katy's the person you'd be substituting for. When she can't make it here to Carey, you'd play for the dance classes in her place."

Mama kept talking while she wetted her face and neck some more. "Katy goes to the same school as Daddy. The university in Logan. She's in one of Miss Davis's classes at the university."

"Miss Davis?" I asked, looking at Mama. "Who's that?"

"The dance teacher, Lona Davis," Mama said. She started looking at me again. "The other night at dinner, Jazz was telling everybody how she had met the new dance teacher and how pretty she was, remember?"

If I had remembered, I wouldn't have asked who she was.

This time I didn't let what I was thinking fly out like I had before. I only said, "Um," and shrugged my shoulders. Then I turned my head and started staring out into the yard and listening to Jazz's "electric birds."

There's a summer humming in our neighborhood that sounds like buzzing. One time when it started, Jazz said, "Watch out, everybody! Those electric birds are startin' up, but you'd better not get near one. If you do, they'll go 'buzzap' and you'll get a big old shock!"

Daddy explained that it's insects called cicadas making the sound and *not* birds. But Jazz, with her peculiar self, told Daddy *he* was the one making a mistake.

"They *have* to be birds, Daddy," she said. "Bugs can't make all that noise. Not even electric bugs. They're too teeny."

Even though Jazz is the baby of the family—she's nine and only in the fourth grade—and a *huge* pain most of the time, she says things in a way that everybody in the family remembers. Like calling cicadas electric birds. Now all of us talk about the humming sounds being electric birds.

When I left my letter to Clovis to see what Mama wanted, Jazz had been sitting with Mama on the porch. When I came out, Mama had told Jazz to go out in the yard and play so the two of us could talk. She was still there, bouncing up and down and jumping around the yard. She didn't even seem to notice how hot it was. At first I couldn't figure out what she was doing. Then I did. She was dancing.

Jazz is the one they ought to get to be the substitute pianist. She's been wanting to dance forever.

I knew what I was thinking wasn't fair. Jazz can't even play the piano all that much. Plus, the only things she wants to play are tunes she's made up and the boogie-woogie pieces Uncle J. B. is always teaching her.

Maybe I can convince Mama that Jazz should be the one to take the lessons. Yeah...

I looked over at Mama again. She had stopped rubbing ice on herself and was leaning against the porch rail with her eyes shut. "Mama?" I said.

"Ummm?" she said without opening her eyes.

I took a deep breath. I figured it would help me get everything out. "Mama, I'm not tryin' to be difficult like you been sayin' lately that I'm tryin' to be, but I honestly, *honestly* don't want to take those dance classes. But look at Jazz, Mama. Jazz really wants—"

"Ernestine!" Mama cut me off. Then she opened her eyes and looked at me. "Ernestine," she said again, only this time my name didn't sound so loud. "You won't be *taking* dance classes. You'll be playing the piano for the kids who are. And it will only have to be sometimes. Like I explained earlier, you'll be the *substitute* pianist."

"But, Mama, why do I have to be involved with those classes at all?"

My voice had come out louder than I wanted it too. I figured that's why Mama started frowning. Even so, I didn't say "Excuse me."

Mama didn't give me one of her looks or anything. She just put her hand on my arm. It was wet and cold.

"Ernestine," she said, "just hear me out for a minute."

She took a deep breath and started rubbing her hand up and down my arm.

"Miss Helen asked your father and me if it would be okay to ask you to be the substitute pianist for the dance classes," she said. "That was the first thing that happened. And she asked because she has a lot of confidence in you *and* your talent."

Mama took her hand off my arm and rubbed her two hands together. "But that's not the only reason we decided to ask you to think about taking on the responsibility."

I leaned my head back against the porch rail. I could feel the roll of fat on my neck pushing against the top part of my back.

"It wasn't fair of me not to give you the other reason right along with the first one," Mama said, "and I apologize for that."

Mama let out another big breath. "In return for you being the substitute pianist, Jazz would be able to take lessons," Mama said. "You know how much that would mean to her. Jazz wants to take dance classes as much as you *don't* want to. And since we just can't afford it right now with Daddy being back in school and all, the exchange seems like an ideal arrangement."

Ideal for everybody but me!

I didn't say anything. I just kept leaning my head back, looking at Mama's face and feeling my fat.

Mama started brushing her cold fingers across my hair. "Ernestine, I didn't tell you everything right away because I don't think the deal is the thing that matters the most.

Getting lessons for Jazz *is* one of the positive outcomes, but to me the most important thing in all of this is the confidence people are showing in *you*. Confidence in your ability and your talent."

Mama twisted her fingers in the loose hair at the end of one of my plaits. "Whether you believe it or not, baby," she said, "being asked to accompany a dance class is quite an honor for an eleven-year-old."

"Twelve," I said, correcting Mama. "I'll be twelve in two weeks."

"Excuse me," Mama said. This time the "cuse" part was regular. "I stand corrected. But it's also quite an honor for a *twelve*-year-old."

Mama stood up. Then she held out her hand to me, offering to help me up. I took it.

"Can I count on you to at least *think* about helping out the dance classes?" she asked me.

"Un-huh," I said, nodding my head at the same time. I was standing beside Mama, but I didn't look at her when I answered.

"Then, that's good enough for me," she said.

But it's not good enough for me.

I didn't say anything else to Mama before she went back into the house. I just sat there, watching my peculiar little sister and thinking about what Mama had just told me.

Dumb, DUMB dance classes. Only somebody silly like Jazz wants to take them, anyhow.

A picture of my friend Alicia popped into my mind. And then of her evil twin, Edna. And of her next-door neighbor, Amanda. Amanda Nelson Clay.

I thought of the other lessons all of us had been at together—the piano lessons at Miss Elder's. I remembered how Amanda had treated me when I had first started coming for my lessons. How she had called me "Fatso" behind my back.

Another picture popped into my mind. Amanda and Edna and Alicia and all the other skinny girls leaping and twirling and floating in the air. Just like Jazz was doing.

And there I'll be, lumped on the piano bench like a turtle stuck in the mud. The return of Fatso.

The electric birds were getting louder, but I was glad. Maybe the noise would get all the thoughts out of my head. But even if it did, nothing was going to make me stop wishing that I would never have to play the piano again in my whole entire life.

4 ᔯ *Amanda*

JUST WAIT UNTIL I tell Alicia about this. She won't believe it!

I could hardly believe it myself. There I was, huddled behind the couch in our living room, holding my breath so nobody would know I was there. It was too weird to believe.

I had already been on the floor behind the couch when Madelyn and Marcus came in the living room. I had gone there to sit under the window fan. I knew it would be a good place to stay cool while I thought about what to write in my new diary. And it would be someplace private.

I must have been concentrating harder than I thought. I hadn't even heard the doorbell ring. I didn't realize anybody was in the living room but me until I heard talking.

"Oooooweeee, it feels good in here!"

It was Marcus. And I could tell from the sound of his voice that he was close to the couch.

I have to get up so he'll know I'm back here.

I put my diary down and started pressing my hands down on the floor to push myself up when I heard Madelyn's voice. "This should feel good, too," she said. Then I heard a big smack.

She's kissin' him! Madelyn and Marcus are kissin' right here in the living room!

I stopped trying to push myself up. Instead I moved back down to the floor. I even scooched down farther behind the couch than I had been in the first place.

I gotta stay here. If Madelyn sees me, she'll swear I came in here to spy. I just know she will.

If Madelyn thought I had been hiding to spy on her, she would go running to Mother about it. And that's all I needed. Especially these days.

One of the most terrible parts of Mother and Dad's separation has been living with only Mother. Sometimes she acts so weird that I almost wish we lived with *no* parents instead of just one.

Being stuck at home with Mother most of the summer had been terrible. In the first place she kept on telling me how disappointed she was that I hadn't wanted to go back to Camp Castle where I had gone last summer. Then she would get angry every time I said I wanted to stay over at Dad's for a few days. It was like she didn't want me to be at home and wanted me there at the same time. Weird.

Madelyn said it'll probably get better when Mother goes back to work. That's what Mother's going to do when school starts. She'll have a social-work job like the one she had in between the times Madelyn and I were born. Maybe having to go to the social-work office every day will help Mother stay out of my hair.

But she sure won't if Madelyn tells her I was spyin'.

It wasn't like I had *planned* on being there to spy on my sister and her boyfriend. But Madelyn would never believe that I hadn't. Neither would Mother. Not in a zillion years.

Especially if I don't do something right this very minute!

I couldn't decide what to do. Maybe I should shout something. But what? To just say that I was sitting there would be stupid. Maybe it would be better to stand up. So that's what I decided to do.

I reached for my diary. Even though there wasn't anything written in it yet, I had to make sure nobody else would see it. But before I could start getting myself up again, I could feel the back of the couch pushing into my back.

They're sittin' down!

I scooched back down. This time even farther. Then I looked up to see how far from the top of the couch I was.

What if they look over the edge of the couch and find me sitting down here?

I could see the back of their heads and Marcus's elbow. He had it pushed over the edge of the couch. He had his hand on the back of Madelyn's head and was playing in her hair with his fingers.

"Marcus," Madelyn said. It was more like she breathed his name than said it. The last part of it… it just floated.

"Madelyn, my sweet baby." Marcus's voice was even deeper than it usually is. And *sooooo* soft. If I hadn't been right behind them I might not even have heard it.

Then I heard another smack. And then another.

They're makin' out. I'm sittin' here listenin' to my sister and her boyfriend make out. Alicia won't be able to believe her ears when I tell her this.

Just thinking about the look Alicia would get on her face when I told her about this made me smile. It's not that Alicia's really gossipy, but she does always ask me about Madelyn and Marcus. She said one time that she wanted to know because Marcus is her friend Ernestine's brother. But I think it's because Alicia wants to hear about any kind of romantic stuff. She even sneaks romance magazines into her house. Edna said once their mother caught Alicia sitting in the closet reading one.

Marcus and Madelyn have been going with each other since he was in high school. Now he's almost in his second year of college. I didn't think they'd last this long, especially since Marcus goes to a university in Washington, D. C., which is a long way from where we live. Madelyn is still in high school. She'll be a senior, though, and going away to college herself next year. I just know she's thinking about going to the same university Marcus goes to.

The last time Madelyn and I spent the night over at Dad's, I heard him and Madelyn talking about Marcus. I was stretched out on the floor, watching television, so they probably thought I wasn't paying attention. But I heard every word they said. Every word.

"Don't you have any interest in dating other boys, Madelyn?" Dad asked her.

"Dad, I've told you over and over how I feel about Marcus," she said, "and feeling the way I do, it wouldn't even be fair to date anybody else."

"But how can you be so sure, baby?" Dad said. He sounded like he was pleading with her. "You sat out all the important events last year because Marcus was away at college. Like the junior-senior prom—"

"Dad, the junior-senior prom's no big deal."

"It is when you're a senior, honey, and that's what you'll be in the fall."

"I understand what you're saying, Dad," Madelyn said, "but I want you to understand what *I'm* saying."

Madelyn's voice got super soft before she went on. "Dad, I love Marcus. I love him very much."

As soon as I heard that, I put my hand over my mouth. It was the only thing I could think of to do to keep from laughing out loud. But it didn't work. The laughter came out anyhow.

"Mind your business, Amanda," Madelyn said. Then she threw one of the pillows from the couch at me. She wasn't really mad though. I knew from the way her voice sounded and the way the pillow had just sort of tapped on my back and then bounced off.

I hadn't been looking at Dad and Madelyn, and I didn't turn around to look then, either. I just said, "Nobody's interested in your business, Madelyn. It's too boring to even listen to."

But there behind the couch it wasn't like that at all.

Now whether I'm interested or not, I can hear absolutely everything, without even trying!

Marcus started talking. It sounded like his mouth was covered with something, but I was still able to understand him. "Time's runnin' out fast," he said. "Too fast. I'll be headin' back to school before long."

"Don't make me think about it, Marcus," Madelyn said.

I couldn't help picturing Marcus and Madelyn while they talked, especially since I had already seen Marcus's arm sticking out and his hand in her hair. By now Madelyn probably had her head on Marcus's arm and was probably looking up into his face.

"We *have* to think about it," Marcus said, "so we can make plans to see each other. Do you think you'll be able to talk your parents into lettin' you come for homecoming weekend?"

Madelyn did one of her famous long breaths. I didn't have *any* trouble picturing that.

"I'm pretty sure Dad won't object," she said. "I've been feeling him out this summer. You know, paving the way."

Another long breath.

"But Mother's a different story. There's no paving the way with her. We never know what direction Mother might be coming from."

Without really meaning to, I nodded my head, agreeing with what Madelyn said about Mother.

"It's probably the... the separation," Marcus said. "It's got to be enormously hard for all of you. The entire family." His voice had gotten even deeper. And softer.

After that, neither one of them said anything, and I could tell from the sounds that they had started kissing again.

All I could do was sit there and do nothing. But the really weird part was, that's all I really felt like doing. I didn't feel like laughing the way I had over at Dad's when Madelyn was talking about all that romantic stuff.

I thought that maybe it was different now because at Dad's they knew I was there in the living room with them while they were talking. Here, Madelyn and Marcus didn't know I was there. *Right* there.

Like a spy would be.

Knowing that they *didn't* know began to make me feel weird. Sort of bad. Even though it wasn't my fault that they didn't know. But there was something else, too. Things I couldn't stop my mind from wondering about.

I wonder how hard it is to hold your breath while you're kissing a boy.

I kept thinking about how Marcus's voice had sounded the last time he had said something. How gentle it had been. How anybody could tell just from his voice that he loves Madelyn just as much as she loves him.

I wonder how it feels to be in love with a boy.

It was weird, but none of my wondering made me think about some of the things I usually think from knowing about Marcus and Madelyn. Like what might happen if they are so much in love they'll decide to get married. How I would be related to Ernestine Harris if they did.

But I didn't think about any of that. It was weird. And it was getting harder and harder to keep staying there behind the couch and not make a sound.

Why don't they go out in the kitchen like they always do?

Every time Marcus comes over, it isn't too long before he and Madelyn go into the kitchen to get something to eat. One time Mother told Madelyn that Marcus must have a tapeworm because of how hungry he always is. Madelyn got angry even though Mother said she was only kidding. But Marcus can eat a lot.

Hurry up, Marcus. Go feed your tapeworm!

I scooched down farther while I waited, trying to get more comfortable. Then I picked up my new diary. I opened it to the first page again, being super quiet so the pages wouldn't rustle. The pen I had brought with me had rolled across the floor and was near the other end of the couch. If I tried to reach it, I'd probably make too much noise. So I decided to wait.

While I was sitting there, I finally knew what I wanted to write in my diary. I knew *exactly* what. And I would write it as soon as Madelyn and Marcus left and I had privacy again.

August 10, 1957

Dear Diary,

I wonder if it's weird to kiss a boy on the mouth. I also wonder if I have to wait until I'm in love to find out...

5 ❧ Ernestine

JAZZ WAS MAKING me crazy! She kept talking and asking so many questions, I wanted to strangle her!

"Mama, you gonna get me some toe shoes? I want some black ones. Pink ones look dumb. Can you get me some black ones, Mama?"

Jazz was in the backseat of the car. She was leaning up against the driver's seat and talking right into Mama's ear. But Mama didn't seem to mind. At least that's how it looked. She kept driving along and smiling.

Maybe she's ignoring Jazz. That's what I oughta do.

But it was impossible to ignore my sister who wouldn't shut up for a minute. She didn't even care that nobody was saying anything back!

"It's gonna be fun goin' to dancing, huh, Mama. Don't you think so? Do you wish you were goin'? Mama, I bet you went to dancin' when you were little? And that's why you said you were happy I was gonna be takin' lessons, right?"

I turned around from where I was sitting in the front seat to look at Jazz. When she looked back at me, I made a face at her like I was growling. I didn't make any growly sounds, but I hoped the look would make her shut up.

Jazz just stuck her tongue out at me and went back to talking. "Mama, how come they havin' the dance classes way over on Monroe Street? How come they just don't have them at my school? You know, like they had vacation school there this summer?"

I was glad Mama didn't ignore that question because I wanted to know the answer, too. I hadn't asked it because I wasn't going to ask *anything* about those dumb classes that I didn't have to.

"The committee that's sponsoring the dance classes—" Mama started.

"That's doin' what?" Jazz asked, interrupting Mama.

"Sponsoring. Making it possible for the classes to take place," Mama said, explaining to Jazz. "Remember when we were talking about the classes the other day? I told you how a group of women had worked together to get dance classes started."

"Yeah," Jazz said. She got this big grin on her face. "You said all of them had beautiful black daughters like me!"

"*And* Ernestine," Mama said. She smiled and reached over and patted me on my leg. "I have *two* beautiful black daughters."

Yeah, but you're punishin' one of them so the other one can take the dumb classes.

I didn't say out loud what I was thinking, but I sure wanted to.

Mama kept explaining. "Mrs. Clark, who's one of the mothers, found a place on Monroe Street that's ideal for the classes—a building with huge floor space. It was a store at one time."

"Are you gonna always drive us to dance class, Mama?" Jazz asked, starting with her questions again.

We were stopped at a red light. "Either me or your father," Mama said, "even on the days both you and Ernestine come."

"How come you not gonna be comin' all the time, Ernestine?" Jazz asked me. "How come you wanna miss some of the classes?" She kept going without waiting for an answer. "I don't want to miss *any*. Not a single one! Dancin' is gonna be the best thing in the world. How come you plannin' on missin' classes already, huh?"

She was really being a pain! "Talk about whatchu know, Jessie Louise," I said. I called her by her real name to bug her like she was bugging me. "And stop talkin' about somethin' that's none of your business."

"Mama, Ernestine said somethin' bad to me," Jazz started.

"Tellin' you to mind your own business is not somethin' bad, Jessie," I said, cutting her off.

Mama pulled the car over to the curb. I figured she was getting ready to yell at me and Jazz about fussing. But all she said was, "We're here."

I hadn't been to Monroe Street in a long time. Not since I was at Fourth Street Elementary and Clovis and I would go over to Monroe at lunch recess to buy Moon Pies or frozen ice or sour pickles. Although Monroe isn't all that far away from Fourth Street, we usually had to run both ways to get there and back to school before the bell rang. Plus, whenever we were on Monroe Street, we kinda *wanted* to run. Monroe was never a friendly looking street. It was usually strange and empty. In a way it seemed kind of mysterious.

Monroe Street had a lot of buildings instead of houses. But most of the buildings looked dark and empty. And there were some empty lots where buildings had been torn down. It was easy to tell from the junk in the lots—things like bricks and glass and slabs of concrete. There were a few stores still open in some of the buildings, but most of the stores had been closed up. Even the store we had usually gone to at lunch had a "For Sale" sign in the window.

"This street looks lonesome," Jazz said.

I didn't tell Jazz I agreed with her. I didn't say how the street had always looked that way, either. I figured Mama wouldn't want to hear how many times I had been over there with Clovis. *Or* by myself.

"The only thing you need to concern yourself about on Monroe Street is directly in front of you," Mama said.

Right in front of us was one of the big, lonesome buildings. But it looked a little better than most of the others. For one thing, the first floor was all lit up. And the long wide window facing the street looked brand new. There was a sign in the window that said, WELCOME TO THE DAVIS DANCE STUDIO!

"C'mon, my beautiful black daughters," Mama said, leading us to the doorway of the building. She was grinning and so was Jazz.

But I wasn't grinning and didn't plan to, either.

She can make me come here, but she can't make me like it. Not one bit!

"Ernestine, I've heard so much about you! I'm thrilled that you're going to be helping us out."

Miss Davis had grabbed my hand to shake it and was still holding it. I didn't really mind, but I couldn't think of anything to say back. The only thing I could do was smile.

"I really appreciate your taking time to come by today to meet me and Katy. Will you be able to stay for a while and watch the classes?"

It was like something had happened to my tongue. And my face. I just kept smiling and nodding my head.

"Ernestine?" Mama said. Her voice helped my tongue get loose.

"Yes, ma'am," I said. Plus, there wasn't much more I could say, without lying.

Miss Davis let go of my hand and lifted her arm in the air. The way she did it was like a bird might take off.

"Katy," she said, waving her hand. "Can you step over here for a minute? I want you to meet someone."

The girl she called was sitting on the floor with the little kids. It was where Jazz had gone to sit. When the girl got up, some of the kids started saying, "Don't leave, Katy. Stay with us."

"I'll be right back," the girl said. Then she got up from sitting on the floor with her legs crossed without even using her hands to help herself up!

Everybody in here is graceful. I'm gonna be like a lump in this group!

The girl came over to where me and Mama and Miss Davis were standing and shook my hand just like Miss Davis had done. And without waiting for Miss Davis to introduce us.

"You must be Ernestine Harris," she said. "I'm Katy Ferguson, and I have a message for you from a friend of yours."

My tongue got tied up again. All I could think of to do was stand there and smile. I felt like a fool. But Katy didn't seem to notice. She kept talking.

"I was told to tell you that Dolphin Girl better still be on the case," Katy said. Then she smiled at me like the two of us had a secret.

At first I couldn't figure out what she was talking about. Then it hit me! Katy was bringing me a message from Raelynn! Raelynn, my friend from Hilltop where I had gone to camp last summer. Raelynn who was sixteen and my friend!

I couldn't stop myself from busting out laughing. "The message is from Raelynn, right? Raelynn Jefferson." I could feel myself grinning all over the place, but I didn't care at all.

"You guessed it!" Katy said. "Raelynn sends that message—and this!" Katy put her arms around me and gave me a big hug.

Miss Davis and Mama were still standing there, watching me and Katy. Both of them were smiling.

"Mama," I said, "you remember Raelynn. One of my counselors from camp. You know, from Hilltop. Raelynn's the one who taught me how to swim. She made up the name Dolphin Girl for me. Remember? She's the one I told you and Daddy about. The one—"

Mama interrupted me. It's probably a good thing she did. I was beginning to go on and on like Jazz had been doing in the car. "Yes, baby, I know," she said. "I remember all about Raelynn."

Mama smiled at Katy. "I guess you can see you've brought a message of extreme goodwill," she said

"And that's not all I got from Rae," Katy said. "She told me you play a mean piano when you get warmed up." Katy raised her eyebrows when she looked at me. "Based on everything I've heard about you, I think Miss Davis and I have located the best substitute pianist to be found any-where."

"I'm gonna try to be," I said. My cheeks were practically tired from all the grinning, but there didn't seem to be any-thing else I could do.

6 ☞ Amanda

"YOUR CHARIOT AWAITS, my lady!"

Dad bowed like he was a chauffeur and his car was a limousine. I knew he was waiting for me to laugh, but I thought of something better to do.

"You want me to ride in *that*?" I said. I turned up my nose the way you do when you're disgusted. "That car's dirty, George. I hope you don't expect to drive me to my dance class in a dirty car." Then I turned around and started walking in the direction of the house.

I didn't hear my dad say anything, so I kept on pretending I was headed back inside. I was starting to wonder if Dad hadn't known I was only kidding when I felt his hands reaching under my arms to pick me up.

I screamed. "Dad!" But I was laughing, too. "Dad, whadda you doin'?"

"What does it look like I'm doing?" he said. He was holding me up so far from the ground my feet weren't touching the grass. "Since the ungrateful Lady Amanda won't plant her royal bee-hind in the car, I'll have to do it myself!"

By the time Dad got me back to the car both of us were laughing so hard that he had to let me back down.

"The Lady Amanda is bigger than I thought," Dad said. He let go of my arm and stepped back. "As a matter of fact, she's a *lot* bigger than she used to be."

Dad acted like he hadn't seen me in a long time. "Girl, you're sprouting up like the proverbial weed," he said, looking me up and down. "If you don't stop, you're going to be as tall as me. And almost as fine!"

I knew Dad was teasing me, but I couldn't stop myself from laughing. "Dad, quit it," I said. "Stop being so conceited. And you just saw me day before yesterday. I haven't grown since then."

"As tall as you're getting, you must be doing some growin' every hour," he said. Then after he opened the car door on my side and I started getting in, he pushed my head down like I had gotten super tall.

"Dad, you're actin' like a nut," I said.

"I am. I'm nuts over you," he said, and started whistling.

Dad sure is in a good mood.

Usually Mrs. Raymond, Alicia and Edna's mother, was going to be the one to drive us to dance class. That's what she and Mother decided, since Monroe Street was a little far for us to have to walk. And Mother said she wasn't all that comfortable in the first place about us walking by ourselves on Monroe Street.

AMANDA

"It's desolate over there," she had said.

I wasn't sure what Mother meant, and I knew if I asked she'd tell me to look it up. And I didn't care that much. I was just glad that since the Raymonds had gone away overnight to see Dr. Raymond's mother who was in the hospital, Dad was the one to take me to dance class this week. If Mother had taken me she would be complaining about the "desolate street" the entire time we were on our way.

Dad kept on whistling while he backed the car out of the driveway and started down the street.

"Whatchu so happy about?" I asked him.

"Why do I have to be happy *about* something?" Dad said, grinning. "Can't I be just a happy kind of guy? Hope so, 'cause that's just what I am. Aren't you a happy kind of gal?"

Dad was really acting silly, but I couldn't stop myself from laughing at him. And anyhow, it felt good to be with a parent in a really good mood.

"I guess I am a happy kind of gal," I said. "Especially since I'm on my way to dance class."

"Ah, the great dance class! The new love of your life."

"Dad, don't be ridiculous." It sounded like Dad was beginning to make fun of me.

"I'm serious," he said. "It seems that you really love the dance classes. Am I wrong about that?"

"Nope, you're right," I said. "The classes are terrific!"

We had only had two real classes so far, and both of them had been in the church basement. The same place where we had gone for the meetings about the dance classes. This was the first time our class was going to be in the place Miss Davis said they had rented for the classes.

43

"So, tell me about them," Dad said.

"Well, everything about them is terrific. I even like our dance outfits that Edna calls pukey puce."

"Your outfits are *puce?*" Dad turned up his nose the same way Edna had. "I have to agree with Edna on that one."

"They're not so bad," I said. I smiled to myself.

Especially on me.

"So what else is terrific other than the puce outfits," Dad wanted to know. "For example, the teacher. What's she like?"

"She's *absolutely* terrific, Dad," I said. And she was. In our first real dance class everybody was impressed with Miss Davis. Even Edna.

"She's tall and so thin she's almost skinny. But she's not skinny. She's just... just really cool looking. And everything she does is graceful. Even the way she walks around when she's not dancing."

"Sounds like Miss Davis ranks high on your list," Dad said.

"She's super. Just wait 'til you meet her." Then I thought about something. "Hey, Dad, why don't you stay for a little while and watch part of our class? Then you can meet Miss Davis."

And see how good I already am. Even Miss Davis thinks so.

I didn't say anything about how Miss Davis had told me I had real promise. She said that to me after our last class. And she hadn't said it to everybody. Alicia and Edna said she had told them she was glad they were going to be in her class, but nothing about what kind of dancers they were going to be. Nothing about *them* having promise.

"I do plan to come in and meet your teacher, but I won't be able to stick around. I have a client coming in at four."

Dad's business hours are different on different days. Sometimes he even has to meet with people in the evenings. He says being a lawyer means sometimes he has to meet with clients at times they are off from work. His business hours were one of the things he and Mother used to argue about.

I wonder if I would care if my husband had office hours in the evening?

I told Dad more about the dance classes while we drove to Monroe Street. How the classes for the little kids were going to be held just before the classes for kids my age, and how Miss Davis was really good with the little kids just like she was with us.

"Alicia and I got there last week in time to see part of the little kids' class," I told Dad, "and you shoulda seen what she was able to get those little kids to do. They were walking around that church basement, movin' from side to side without missin' a beat. One little kid was even singin' the blues like the record that was playin'."

"The kids were dancin' to blues music?" Dad asked.

"Yeah," I said. "Miss Davis said we're gonna be dancin' to blues music and spirituals and the drums from Africa and Haiti and—"

"Hmmm," Dad said while I was still talking. But not like he was trying to cut me off. "It sounds like Miss Davis might be a protégé of Katherine Dunham."

"A *what?*"

Dad laughed. "Protégé," he said again. He pronounced it the way he does when he wants me to get a new word in my vocabulary, saying it real slow, like it has really *loooong* sylla-bles. "Someone who's been taught or influenced by a special person. And it sounds as if your Miss Davis has been influ-enced by Katherine Dunham who has spent most of her dance career celebrating the movements and rhythms of black people all over the world."

Sometimes I can't believe how smart my dad is. He knew about Katherine Dunham even before I had a chance to tell him what I already knew. I was going to say something about him knowing so much, but if I did I knew he would keep on telling me stuff, and I really wasn't *that* interested.

By the time he finished explaining about Katherine Dunham, we were finally there. On Monroe Street that has a lot of old, ugly buildings. Dad was parking in front of one with a sign that said WELCOME TO THE DAVIS DANCE STUDIO! It wasn't at all like I had expected the dance stu-dio to look.

Desolate must mean deserted, 'cause that sure is how this street looks.

Dad looked at me like he was reading my mind. "What's the matter?" he asked me.

"It's just not what I had expected," I said.

"What did you expect?"

I started thinking about the dance school on Merritt Avenue. It's where the white kids take ballet and the school our parents had tried to get a teacher from last year. The dance school on Merritt is painted pink. It even has a pink awning that has "Dance on Merritt" written on it. You can't see how it looks inside because of the lace curtains at the window.

Dad and I were standing in front of the window that had Miss Davis's sign plastered across it, but I could still see inside. There wasn't much in the room at all. Not even a rail across the wall like dance studios are supposed to have. The room was huge. And one wall had a mirror across most of it. But the other walls looked dull. Sort of gray.

Miss Davis must like boring colors.

The little kids' class was still going cn. They were sitting on the floor with a woman who wasn't Miss Davis, but she was moving her arms in the air like a dancer would.

"…a tragedy."

I had been concentrating so hard on trying to see inside that I hadn't heard everything Dad had said. "Huh?" I asked him.

"I said Monroe Street is a tragedy. A no-man's-land between the black and white communities of Carey."

I didn't know what Dad was talking about, and I didn't really have time to find out. Anyhow, I could tell from the way he was talking that his explanation was going to be one of those long history things.

I grabbed his hand. "C'mon, Dad. Let's go inside so you can meet Miss Davis before you have to go."

"At your service, Lady Amanda," Dad said. But he stopped to look through the window like I had been doing.

"Isn't that Marcus's sister over there?" he said.

"What?" I turned back to look through the window again. "Where?"

"Over there," Dad said, pointing.

I followed Dad's finger, expecting to see Jazz, sitting with the group of little kids. Ernestine had told me last year that

Jazz wanted to take dance lessons and that she didn't. Not at all. Alicia had told me Ernestine had told her the same thing.

She probably doesn't want to put on one of the dance outfits. They show everything.

Then I saw Jazz. But it wasn't where Dad was pointing.

"Over by the piano," he said, still pointing. "That girl looks like Ernestine. Yes, it is she."

It *was* Ernestine. And it looked like she was playing what the little kids were listening and moving to.

"Hmmm," Dad said. "Using a young person as her pianist. I think I like this Miss Davis already."

"Hmmm," I said, too. Then I yanked Dad's hand hard so he would follow me into the building.

7 ↝ Ernestine

I COULD TELL by the way Mr. Jackson backed out the kitchen door of the restaurant that he was holding something in front of him. I could also see lights flickering.

I bet it's my birthday cake!

I had figured right! Mr. Jackson walked to our table, holding a big caramel cake with twelve candles on it. At the same time everybody at our table started singing "Happy Birthday." It seemed like the whole entire restaurant was singing. But when it got to the part of the song Jazz always makes up, I could hear her above everybody.

> *You look like my sister.*
> *And you smell like her, too!*

We all busted out laughing. Even Mama who gets upset

with Jazz sometimes when she acts up in public.

"You gonna blow out all those candles?" Jazz asked after Mr. Jackson put down the cake in front of me.

"Yeah," I said. "It's *my* birthday." I pointed to the name written in yellow letters on the cake. "See?" I said. "It says 'Ernestine.'"

"Then you better not make your wish too important," Jazz said, leaning as close to the cake as she could get without setting her hair on fire. "'Cause you not gonna be able to blow out all them candles with one breath."

Mama and Daddy were looking at me, but they didn't say anything. I figured they were waiting for me to tell Jazz to get her face out of my cake.

Jazz's face was so close to mine I could look into her eyes and see the lights from the candles. Her eyes were shimmery, making the lights move around.

It's like lights are dancin' in her eyes.

I looked at Jazz and smiled. "You know, Jazz," I said, "you might be right. I think you better help me. Then we'll have two breaths to blow them out."

It was like I had given Jazz a dollar or something. She got this big smile on her face and said, "Yay!"

"But *I'm* the only one who can make a wish, okay?"

"Okay."

I had already decided what I was going to wish for, so I just closed my eyes and said it again to myself.

Please let Clovis come back from Georgia by Christmas.

As soon as I opened my eyes I said, "Okay, let's go!"

Jazz took in a big breath and puffed out her cheeks, then we blew together.

"Yay!" Jazz said again. "We did it!"

"Thanks, li'l sis," I said. I looked at Marcus and winked. I figured he would know that I was calling Jazz by the same name he calls me sometimes—li'l sis. I figured I was right when he winked back.

Mr. Jackson handed me a knife. It was long and silver with a yellow ribbon tied around it. I looked up at him.

"It's customary for the birthday lady to cut the first slice," he said. "And then, if you would like, I'll serve the rest."

"Wow," I said. It was all I could think of to say.

I'm gonna write Clovis about this as soon as I get home.

I had figured nothing would be amazing about my birthday this year. That's what I had told Marcus one day while we were walking down Jackson Street, on our way home from the grocery store. I had been complaining about how much work it always takes for the big family party we have whenever anybody in the family has a birthday.

"It's not that the parties aren't fun. It's just that they're so much work. Even for the person whose birthday it is. And it's so hot this August! It's even too hot for Daddy to barbecue his famous ribs."

When Marcus said, "I agree," I almost fell over. I was waiting for him to tell me it was never too hot for Daddy's ribs. Everybody in the family loves them, but Marcus practically kills himself eating them up.

"I think a celebration for someone turning twelve should be something extra special," he said. "Like a party at the Jackson Street Cafe."

"Yeah, that *would* be special." I laughed. Marcus was only saying that because we were coming up to the restaurant right then. "With all the money they *don't* have to burn, Mama and Daddy are just dyin' to give me a party at the Jackson Street Cafe."

"I know money's tight," Marcus said, "and a party here won't be cheap."

Marcus had stopped in front of one of the front windows of the restaurant. There wasn't anybody inside eating. Probably because it wasn't even evening yet. I had looked in lots of times, but I had never gone inside. But I had always wanted to. The Jackson Street Cafe is the only fancy restaurant in Carey that black people can go to. Plus, it's owned by black people.

My face was so close to the window my nose touched the glass. "It looks nice inside even when it's empty," I said. "Have you ever eaten here, Marcus?"

Marcus started smiling. Like he was remembering something special. "Yeah," he said. I could tell he was trying to keep his smile from getting too big. "Madelyn took me out to dinner here just before I went away to college last year."

I bet Amanda's been here, too. The Clays don't have to worry about havin' enough money.

I turned away from the window. "C'mon, Marcus," I said. "We can forget about me havin' a birthday party here for sure."

"Not so fast, li'l sis," he said. He caught hold of my arm to keep me from moving away. "Mama and Dad want to do something special for your birthday," he said, "and since you're not too big of a pain for a li'l sis, so do I."

I figured Marcus had been fooling me while we were standing there in front of the restaurant. But it turned out that he wasn't! He said that helping to pay the restaurant bill was going to be part of his birthday present to me. And when I said something to Mama about how going to a restaurant was going to be too expensive for everybody, she said it wasn't polite to talk about how much a gift was going to cost. And when she said she was going to invite my friend Alicia to come, too, it seemed like it was too good to be true.

But it was true. It was even turning out to be the best birthday party I ever had in my whole entire life.

After I cut the first slice of cake, I handed the fancy knife back to Mr. Jackson.

"Who you gonna serve that piece to, Ernestine?" Jazz asked.

"Why, you, of course."

Jazz was so surprised when I handed her the piece of cake, she got this look on her face like she couldn't think of anything else to say. Everybody laughed, including me.

Then Daddy stood up. He tapped his water glass with his spoon. In the Jackson Street Cafe, they use fancy goblets for the water. Daddy's tapping on his glass made bell sounds.

"May I have your attention, please?" Daddy said.

He lifted up his glass. "I want to make a toast," he said. "A toast to my daughter."

Everybody got quiet and reached for their glass. Everybody except me, because I didn't think I was supposed to.

Daddy looked at me. His eyes were kinda shimmery like Jazz's had been. "To my beautiful daughter, Ernestine," he said, lifting his glass higher into the air. "Happy August 18, sweetheart, the day of your birth. May the many, many, *many* birthdays ahead bring you the full measure of joy you bring to your mother and me!"

Marcus said, "Hear, hear!" Then everybody else said the same thing. Even Jazz. And without being a pain at all.

After everyone had taken a sip out of their glasses, Alicia leaned over and whispered, "Ernestine, you're so lucky. Nobody's ever toasted me."

I could tell from her shimmery eyes that Alicia was glad for me. Plus, that's the way she is.

I raised up my glass. "I'll toast you now," I said. "To Alicia. May the—"

Jazz butted in before I could finish. "And to Jazz," she started saying, "may the many, many, many, many, *many* birthdays ahead bring you all the toys and strawberry short-cakes and diamond jewels and…"

Jazz kept going on and on, being a pain as usual. But I didn't mind. My birthday party had been so amazing that even Jazz interrupting me to toast herself wasn't going to mess it up.

"Ernestine, don't stay up too late," Mama called to me from the bottom of the stairs.

"I won't. 'Night, Mama."

I was upstairs in Mama and Daddy's room where I had gone to get a piece of Mama's stationery. I had used all of mine and didn't want to open the new box I got for my birthday until my birthday was completely over. *And* I wanted to write to Clovis before I went to bed, which was going to have to be *before* midnight.

On my way back to my room I had to pass by Mama's full-length mirror. I had been planning to close my eyes when I walked by. *Not* looking at myself in that no-love mirror was what I had been doing ever since I got back from Grandmother Carroll's, where Jazz and I had spent most of the summer.

And where I ate like I thought food was gonna disappear forever!

Before I got to the door one of the sheets of stationery slipped out of my hand and fell under the mirror. When I reached down to pick it up, I couldn't stop from seeing myself in the mirror. And because I was so close, I saw myself good.

The bumps that had started growing on my forehead seemed even bigger than they had been that morning. Plus, it looked like a new one was popping out on my cheek. When I turned my head sideways to get a closer look at the new one, I noticed that my behind was taking up almost all of the space in the mirror!

Geez! It's gettin' so big!

While I stood there, I remembered what I had seen in the other mirror I had stared into lately. The one at Miss Davis's dance studio.

The mirror opposite where I had been sitting at the piano was enormous. It ran across practically the entire wall. Most of what I could see of myself was only my face and shoulders. That was because I was sitting down. But I could see every part of the other girls while they were out on the floor. Girls that were the same age as me.

And almost every single one of them is thin!

Thinking about the girls in the dance class made a picture of Amanda come into my mind. How she looked better in her dance things than almost anybody else. She looked so good that I'd almost been staring at her. That's why I noticed that she was already kind of a good dancer, too. And the classes hadn't even been going on all that long.

Amanda's so mean sometimes. It's not fair for her to be so lucky.

I stuck out my tongue at the mirror. But it was already too late. Mama's no-love mirror and the pictures in my head were making me remember everything.

How I would have to watch all the skinny Minnies jump around whenever I played for those dumb dance classes.

Even Alicia. I'll probably wind up hatin' her!

How all the seventh-grade girls except me would be thin.

And they'll probably all get boyfriends…

And how Daddy had made his toast.

To my beautiful daughter, Ernestine…

"You shoulda said your FAT daughter, right, Daddy?"

I had whispered the words, but they were screaming inside my head.

It wasn't midnight yet, but I knew my birthday was over. I ran away from Mama's mirror and into the bathroom. Jazz might still be awake in our room, and I didn't want to talk to anybody.

I sat on the edge of the tub so I wouldn't be able to see into the mirror above the sink in case I looked in that direction accidentally. To make doubly sure, I looked down at my hands. That's when I saw the writing paper I had taken from Mama's desk. I had been holding it so hard it had gotten all wrinkled up.

Plus, now I can't even talk to Clovis…

8 ☙ Amanda

"AMANDA? MADELYN? Are you coming down?"

It sounded like Mother was already on her way up the stairs even though she had told us to come down to the living room. I opened my bedroom door to see where she was *and* to keep her from coming all the way up. If she came into my bedroom and saw what a mess it was, she would start carrying on. It wouldn't make any difference to her that I would be cleaning it up tomorrow like I did every Saturday.

When I leaned over the banister, I saw Mother on the next-to-bottom step. "I'm on my way," I said, hoping to stop her from coming any farther.

"See what's holding up your sister," she said.

"Madelyn!" I yelled in the direction of Madelyn's room. "C'mon."

"I could have done that, Amanda," Mother said. It was

more like she spit it out than said it. Then she turned around and went back down the stairs.

"Sorry," I said, making my voice super soft.

And I hope that was too soft for you to even hear because I'm really not sorry.

I went to Madelyn's door and opened it without knocking. She was so near the door, it would have hit her if she hadn't jumped back.

"Amanda? What are you doin'?"

"Comin' to see what's holdin' you up," I said in the same sort of evil-sounding voice she had used. "Just like Mother told me to do."

Madelyn stood there looking at me without saying anything. Then she closed her eyes and started moving her head from side to side like she was trying to shake something out of it. "Sorry, Amanda," she said. "I didn't mean to snap at you."

"I'm glad," I said, "because Mother snaps enough for everybody!" I felt like plopping down on Madelyn's bed but I knew I couldn't. We had to get downstairs before Mother called us again. Even so, I couldn't make myself turn around and start moving.

"What's this all about anyhow?" I asked Madelyn. "What does Mother want to talk to us about?"

It seemed like Madelyn was stuck in place the same way I was. She hadn't moved, either. She still didn't when she answered me. She didn't even open her eyes.

"She wants to tell us *the* decision," she said with her eyes closed.

"*The* decision?" I was getting ready to ask Madelyn what

the she was talking about when suddenly I knew.

Mother's going to tell us what she and Daddy are going to do. Whether they're going to stay separated or not.

My eyes closed like Madelyn's were. And I wasn't trying to do what she was doing. They just closed by themselves.

Please, please, PLEASE let the decision be good.

Before I knew what I was doing, I started putting a spell on myself. It was something I hadn't done in a zillion years! When I was a little kid I had done it a lot to make things happen. I would tell myself things like, "If I hold my breath until the hand on the clock moves all the way around, Mother will bake the chocolate cake like she promised."

I almost couldn't believe it, but I was doing the same thing while I stood in Madelyn's room. I was putting a spell on myself, saying that the longer I kept my eyes shut, the better the decision would be.

Then I started thinking how weird I probably looked, standing there in the middle of the floor with my eyes shut. How weird Madelyn and I *both* probably looked. Imagining this made me open my eyes.

Madelyn was still standing there, staring at me. I stared back at her. Neither of us said anything. We didn't have to. I knew exactly how she was feeling and that she knew the same thing about me.

"Bet you're hopin' what I'm hopin'," I said to Madelyn. "Right?"

Madelyn smiled. Sort of. She nodded her head.

"And Mother and Dad *have* been gettin' along lately, don't you think?" I said, still staring at Madelyn.

Madelyn nodded her head again. Sort of.

I took a deep breath.

Maybe if I hold my breath until Dad comes, everything will turn out okay.

I made myself let the breath out.

"Madelyn, you know something I don't know, don't you?" I said.

Madelyn looked down at her feet. Then she looked back at me. "No, Amanda," she said. "I don't. I really don't. I only…"

"You only what? *What?*"

Madelyn reached for my hand. "C'mon," she said. "Let's get downstairs like Mother asked us to."

I squeezed her hand hard. I wanted to make her finish saying what she had started. "Only *what*, Madelyn?"

Madelyn turned to look at me. "I only…I just think we shouldn't get our hopes up. That's all."

Before I could say anything back to her, Madelyn pulled me with her while she started down the stairs.

It was dark outside. The only lights on in the living room were the floor lamps by the couch, and they were turned on low. The air blowing in from the window fan was cooler than it had been all week. Probably because it had rained earlier. But it still seemed so hot in the room I almost couldn't breathe.

I'm gonna suffocate to death and fall over.

When we came into the living room, Mother was sitting in the middle of the couch. She patted the cushions next to her the way you do when you want someone to sit beside you. But I sat on the floor in front of the couch and Madelyn sat in a chair across the room.

Mother looked weird, sitting by herself between the two lamps. The lights shining on her face made it look like a smile had been painted under her nose. The smile stayed the same even when she started talking.

"Your father was supposed to be here. I expected him over an hour ago." Mother looked up at the clock on the mantle before she went on. "He *said* he wanted to be a part of this conversation, and *I* certainly wanted him to, but he must have had something else more important to do."

Mother's words snapped like they had done when she was on the stairs. I wanted to ask her what she meant about Dad and to make my words snap the same way when I did. I didn't though. Anyhow I was still having trouble catching my breath.

Madelyn cleared her throat. "Mother," she said, "we don't mind waiting for Dad. We can—"

Mother cut her off. "There's no need to keep putting this off. No need at all!"

She got up and walked behind the couch. She stopped in front of the window fan. I thought she was going to turn it off.

No, please! I'll pass out for sure.

She started talking again without turning back around. Her voice was low and the window fan was still humming. I had trouble hearing what she said.

I looked over at Madelyn who shrugged her shoulders. She acted like she didn't know what Mother had said either. And like she didn't care.

"What did you say, Mother?" I asked.

Mother turned around. She looked at me almost like I was a stranger or something. Then she walked back to the couch and sat down in the exact same place where she had been sitting before.

Finally she answered my question. "I said, your father and I are getting a divorce. Actually, I'm sure this comes as no surprise. Your father has probably already said something to you about it. Maybe that's why he hasn't bothered—"

"Don't talk about Dad like that!"

Madelyn's voice was loud when she cut Mother off. It wasn't exactly yelling but almost. But Mother didn't say anything. She didn't even tell Madelyn not to use that tone with her like I expected her to do. She just kept sitting there with the weird smile on her face.

The divorce smile.

"I'm not talking about your father in any way," Mother said, looking right at Madelyn. "I merely said—"

Madelyn cut Mother off again! I couldn't believe it!

"I heard what you said, Mother! I've heard every single word. And you're not being fair. In the first place it wasn't fair for you not to wait for Dad to get here."

This time Mother didn't keep sitting. Or smiling. She got up off the couch and pointed her finger at Madelyn. "Now see here, young lady—" she started. But she was cut off again. This time by the doorbell.

A key turned in the lock and the door opened. I knew without turning around to look that it was Dad.

"Well. You finally decided to join us," Mother said with her snappy words.

The suffocating began to get really bad.

"I'm sorry to be so late," Dad said. He kept walking into the living room until he got next to Mother. "I should have called."

"Yes, you should have," Mother said. None of her words moved up and down. Her voice sounded like it was stuck on one note.

"There was so much confusion over there. I should have left sooner, I know, but I was trying to find out what happened...trying to help..." Dad started shaking his head like what he was saying didn't make any sense to him just like it didn't to us.

"George, what are you talking about? What's wrong?" Mother said.

"Monroe Street," Dad said. "There was, ah...a big commotion on Monroe Street tonight."

Commotion?

"I thought some people might have gotten hurt..."

Hurt?

Madelyn got up and walked over to where Mother and Dad were standing. She started asking Dad a lot of questions like Mother was doing. Except her questions were about one thing, and Mother's were about another.

"Where on Monroe Street? Anywhere near the dance studio?" Madelyn asked.

"You might at least have called us, George. Suppose we had heard about it and wondered if that's where you were?" Mother asked.

"Dad, answer me! *Was* anyone hurt?"

"You were supposed to be here, talking with the girls. Why were you over on Monroe Street?"

"Who was over there, Dad? Anybody we know?"

"Was it more important for you to be over there than over here?"

I couldn't stand it anymore. Especially the suffocating. It was making me have so much trouble breathing that I had to take breaths with my mouth open to get any air at all. And that made a *lot* of noise. But nobody noticed. They weren't paying *any* attention to me!

I hate you! I hate ALL of you!

I wanted to scream at them, but the only thing I did was get up and run to the steps leading upstairs. And *that's* when all three of them started paying attention. The reason I knew was because suddenly it got super quiet.

None of you would care if I died!

I didn't stop running until I got to my bedroom. Then I went inside and slammed the door as hard as I could.

9 ☣ *Ernestine*

August 19, 1957

Dear Clovis,

I have so much to tell you in this letter, I don't even know where to begin. I'm sitting here trying to figure out what you would want to hear about first, and I can't even decide that! Plus, I have to finish this letter before I leave my room again because when Mama sees me she's going to dream up a whole bunch of things for me to do.

I looked over at the bedroom door to make sure it was shut. If it was, maybe nobody would bust in to bother me.

It's so hard to have someplace private in this house!

When I went over to check the door to make sure the latch had caught, I decided to put a chair up against the doorknob. This was the only way we could kinda lock the door since the key had disappeared. Then I went back to the desk.

I think you would want to hear the most exciting news first. I probably shouldn't call it exciting since it's not really good news, but it really IS exciting. And since nobody got hurt like everybody thought at first, I figure I can say that not all of it is bad news. Just some of it.

I could picture Clovis reading what I had written so far and starting to frown up. He would say something like, "So *what* is it?" I could almost hear his voice in my head.

Okay, okay. I know you can't wait to find out, so I'll get to the point. Remember in my last letter when I told you about the new dance studio on Monroe Street and how it was near the store we used to go to when we were at Fourth Street? You know what? Last night somebody busted into the studio AND the store AND a bunch of other buildings on Monroe. Just busted in and tried to wreck everything they could. Plus, whoever did it didn't even steal anything!

I stopped writing. It felt like I needed to give Clovis a minute to take in all this news. I knew he would be as shocked as I had been when Uncle J. B. had come by this morning after breakfast to tell us what had happened.

Uncle J. B. was the one who came by to tell us. He had gone past Monroe Street on his way home from my BIRTH-DAY DINNER AT THE JACKSON STREET CAFE.

66

I laughed out loud while I was writing about my birthday party all in capital letters.

I bet Clovis will think I'm foolin' him.

To make certain he knew I was telling the truth about being at the restaurant, I was going to put a paper napkin from the restaurant in the letter. I had saved the one they gave me when they served my ginger ale before dinner. It had "Jackson Street Cafe" written on it.

Thinking about how much I had to tell him about my party made me want to hurry up and finish the part about what happened on Monroe Street.

Uncle J. B. said he turned down Monroe when he saw the flashing lights from the police cars and ambulance. He said there was a river of broken glass. Those were his exact words. Isn't it amazing to imagine a river of glass? The ambulance was there because they just knew with all that glass that somebody had to have gotten hurt. But the really amazing thing is that nobody did.

I remembered how Mama had looked when Uncle J. B. was telling us about the glass part. How she had put both of her hands on the sides of her face and looked like she was ready to cry. Then she had looked at Jazz and me. She didn't say anything, but from her face I think she might have been thinking about me and Jazz going to Monroe Street for those dance classes. About what might have happened if a dance class had been going on when the glass river started flowing.

Both Daddy and Uncle J. B. said what happened on Monroe Street was vicious vandalism. Those were their exact words, too. And I, the great Ernestine, explained to my young sister Jazz what vandalism means. (She already knew what vicious means, which is no surprise.) I kept asking who had done all the vandalism. Every time I did, Uncle J. B. and Daddy shook their heads. But they kinda looked at each other, too. I think they're not telling us everything they know.

I read over everything I had written so far to make sure I told Clovis everything about Monroe Street he would want to know.

Marcus is going to drive me and Mama and Jazz over to Monroe Street tomorrow so we can see what happened for ourselves. I'll write you again the very second I find out more about this mystery.

I drew a sign with "The End of Bad News" written on it. I wanted to let Clovis know I was getting to the good part of the letter.

And it *was* good! Telling Clovis about the party kinda made it happen all over again. I tried to remember every single detail. I even told him how I had seen Uncle J. B. holding Mrs. Vines's hands at the table when they thought nobody was looking.

I think Uncle J. B. and Mrs. Vines are...

I started to write "in love." Then I changed my mind. *Clovis might think I'm bein' mushy.*

...like each other a lot.

I thought about Uncle J. B. and Mrs. Vines and how they had been looking at each other. How their eyes had been shimmery practically the whole night. And how looking at them had made me feel...

Then I remembered something else.

YIKES! If Uncle J. B. decides to marry Frankie Vines like Marcus might marry Madelyn, I'll be related to Amanda Clay TWO ways. But maybe not. Does it count when somebody's your godmother and not related by blood? But no matter what, if Marcus and Madelyn don't break up, I'll still be stuck with Amanda as a practically relative!!!!!

I drew a face with the eyes crossed. But I smiled at the same time. Clovis would know I didn't really feel as bad as it sounded in the letter.

Amanda's not so bad. A little, but not an enormous amount...

What I was thinking made me smile more.

The birthday cake was so enormous that I was able to bring a big hunk home. There's still some left over, even after Jazz and I both had a slice for breakfast and I had a big piece after I got home from the restaurant.

A picture of what I had seen in the mirror when I had gone to Mama's room to get a piece of stationery popped into my head. I remembered how I had felt when I saw myself. Then I erased everything I had written about the cake.

I think I've told you everything. Wait! I haven't asked you anything! If I don't, you'll think I don't care what's happening down there in good old Georgia. But I'll have to ask fast because Jazz'll be home soon from her friend Evette's and driving me crazy as usual, so here goes: Howareyoufeeling? Haveyoumetanynewkidsyet? Hasyourdadgotten hisnewcarlikehesaidhewasgoingto? Tellmeeverythinginyournext letter!

By the time I finished the run-together words and sentences, I was laughing out loud. There was only one thing left to say.

Love,
Ernestine

10 ❧ *Amanda*

August 23, 1957

Dear Diary,

I can't believe how right Godmother Frankie was when she said I would want to write to you every day! You are the absolute best secret keeper I could find in a zillion years! Even better than Alicia. And I can tell you that because I know you'll never tell her. Right? Right.

I could see myself in my long mirror while I was writing. I tried not to notice, but it was hard. I could see every movement I made out the corner of my eye without even *trying* to watch.

I can tell you anything. Even how I like seeing myself in the mirror. If I told that to Alicia she would think I was conceited. She might not say it, but I know she would think it, even though she's a terrific best friend. But I'm not conceited. I just like seeing myself these days. Especially now that I'm learning how to express myself with my body. Does that sound weird to you? It did to me at first, but Miss Davis says that's something every dancer has to learn to do.

I remembered some of the things Miss Davis had shown us in our last class. And how after she asked us to try it out, she had told me I caught on fast. Then I remembered why it might be a long time before we could have another class and I could catch on fast about anything.

Whoever did all that wrecking on Monroe Street broke all the windows at the dance studio. Even the mirrors that were along the wall. I HATE whoever it was!!! The only thing I know is it had to be somebody really stupid. SUPER stupid!!!! Who else would wreck something for no reason? I'm just sorry whoever it was didn't slip and fall down in the glass that was all over the street. You wouldn't believe how much there was. Falling into that much glass would have cured the wrecker from doing any more damage, anywhere!

It started getting cloudy outside. I moved to the other end of the bed so I could see better.

It looks like it's getting ready to rain. If it does, I hope it ends before tomorrow so the cookout at the Harrises won't be messed up. Can you believe I said that? It's weird, but I don't hate it at all that I have to go with Madelyn and Dad. We're invited because the cookout is a farewell party for Marcus. He's going back to college next week. Mother was invited, too, but she's not going. I'm even glad I'm going. And I would never tell that to anybody but you. It's not that I want to be with Ernestine or anybody else in her family. But the last time I went to the Harrises for a cookout I had a really good time.

I remembered Ernestine's birthday party that I had gone to last summer after I got back from camp. That had been a cookout, too.

Maybe Billy Carson will be there this time like he was before. I saw him downtown the other day and he has really gotten cuter. And he was never all that bad.

It was getting so dark and cloudy outside, I reached over to turn on the light beside my bed.

I think I'll wear my new red dress tomorrow. It's one of the outfits I got to wear when school starts, but it's good for a cookout, too. Mother will probably tell me to wear something old since I'm going to be outside and eating picnic stuff.

I could hear Mother's voice inside my head. "Why are

you wearing that, Amanda?" she'd say. Only it really wouldn't be a question. What she would really be saying was, "You shouldn't be wearing that, Amanda. Don't you know better than to wear your new clothes to a cookout?"

Sometimes I really don't like her at all. Sometimes I even think I almost hate her. Please don't think that's terrible. But she does things to make people feel that way. And sometimes that makes it awful to be around her. And I know the way she is is why Dad decided he didn't want to be here anymore.

I stopped writing and looked out the window. The clouds were so dark it was almost like night outside.

I wonder if it will feel different after they get divorced. It can't feel any worse than it does now. Madelyn says that knowing will make it better. But how would she know? Anyhow, she's got Marcus to make her feel better.

I remembered being behind the couch that time, listening to Marcus and Madelyn. They had talked a lot about how hard it was going to be for them to be separated when Marcus went back to school. Marcus kept telling Madelyn to not forget that he would always be there for her.

Madelyn's lucky. She can feel better just thinking about Marcus.

The night Mother told us about the divorce, Madelyn was the one who came up to my room after I ran upstairs. I hadn't wanted to talk to anybody. Especially Mother and Dad. I hadn't even wanted to talk to her.

I had been lying on the bed with my head down in my pillows. Madelyn sat down next to me and started rubbing my back. I knew she thought I was crying, but I wasn't.

"It's gonna be okay, Amanda," she said. "It really is. You probably can't believe this right now, but the worst of it is starting to be over."

"How do you know that?" I said. I was talking right into the pillow, but I knew Madelyn could still hear me. "You don't know how I'm feelin'!"

Madelyn kept rubbing my back. "Amanda, my parents are getting divorced, too. Remember?" she said.

I didn't say anything.

"And we'll still have both Mother and Dad," she said. "We just won't have them in the same place." Madelyn rubbed my arm. "And we'll have each other like we always have. Don't ever forget that. I will always be there for you."

Yeah, like Marcus is always there for you.

After Madelyn said that I had pushed my face farther down in the pillows.

I wish I had somebody like Marcus.

I was getting ready to tell my diary how that somebody should look when I heard running on the stairs. It sounded like Madelyn, but I couldn't be absolutely sure.

It might be Mother soundin' like Madelyn.

I hurried to write one last thing. It was something I did every time at the end of writing in my diary. It was almost like having a spell for my diary.

Gotta go, but you and I know that A.W.R.T.W.D.F.!

Love,
ANC

I locked my diary and put the chain with the key on it back around my neck. Then I put the diary back in the special hiding place no one in the absolute world will ever know of but me.

Somebody might sneak in my room and peek over my shoulder while I'm writing. That's when they'll find out that A.W.R. T.W.D.F. means "anybody who reads this will disintegrate forever!" But they will never EVER ever find my diary without me—Amanda Nelson Clay!

11 ✍ Ernestine

I WISH MAMA would forget my name, FOREVER!

I wanted to say what I was thinking so bad, I almost didn't know what to do! Every time I took a step Mama was calling my name, finding something else for me to do. After she asked me to get some more potato salad from the refrigerator, I was ready to tell her I had already been to the kitchen fifty times! Plus, I was trying as hard as I could to not even *look* at the potato salad. The more I saw it, the more I wanted to eat it.

And I'm not gonna eat any of this food. Even Daddy's ribs. I'm gonna stick to this diet if it kills me.

On my way to the kitchen I saw Jazz. The one time Mama had sent *her* into the kitchen to get something, she had messed up. She had dropped the rolls she was carrying all over the ground. After that Mama didn't ask her to do anything else.

Knowin' Jazz, she might have dropped those rolls on purpose!

I was ready to say something to my sister when Mama called my name again! "Ernestine, please hurry up with that salad, baby." She was standing behind the serving table Daddy and Marcus had set up under the tree. "This bowl is almost empty."

So, let it get empty.

I let the screen door slam behind me when I went into the kitchen.

There was a ton of food still packed into our refrigerator. So much that anybody would think the cookout hadn't even started yet. And people had been gobbling down our food for over an hour.

I had just found the container with the potato salad when the doorbell rang.

One more thing I have to take care of.

At first I couldn't see anybody. Then I saw this long shadow along the porch.

"Wilhelmina!" I said.

Wilhelmina moved in front of the screen door. "Ernestine!" she said. "Hey, girl!"

Wilhelmina had only been back one day from visiting her parents in North Carolina. When she called me to tell me she was back, Mama had answered the phone and invited Wilhelmina to the cookout before she gave the phone to me. I don't know whether I would have invited her or not if Mama hadn't, but seeing her *did* make me glad she was there.

Standing there, practically as tall as a tree, Wilhelmina looked the same as always. She was smiling in this way she has, like she knows something nobody else does. It used to bother me, but I got used to it. And I really *was* glad to see her.

"I was wonderin' where you were," I said. "Everybody else we invited is here."

Wilhelmina walked with me back to the kitchen. "Yeah," she said. "I could see all the people out back when I came down the street. I looked for Alicia, but I didn't see her. Who I *did* see was Amanda Clay."

She was looking at me with one of her eyebrows raised higher than the other. I figured she was waiting for me to tell her why Amanda, who's not really my friend, was at the cookout and why Alicia, who is my friend, wasn't.

Then, before I could decide what I wanted to say back, Wilhelmina answered part of her own question.

"I guess Amanda would *have* to be invited to a cookout being given for her sister's boyfriend," she said.

"Yeah," I said. "I guess." I couldn't think of anything else to say.

"But Alicia would be invited because you *wanted* her to be here, right?"

I was getting ready to tell Wilhelmina that Alicia wasn't there because she had gone with her parents again to the hospital to see her grandmother. But for some reason, I didn't.

I just kept listening to Wilhelmina while I reached into the refrigerator to get the potato salad I had left there when the doorbell rang. Wilhelmina was saying how much she had to tell me about being in North Carolina. How many interesting things she had done, how her parents were teaching at a college, and on and on.

Hearing Wilhelmina kind of talk to herself and watching her peculiar smile made me remember what Mama had said to me about life and colors and people.

Wilhelmina must be filled with all the colors of the rainbow!

I grabbed the potato salad and said, "C'mon, Wilhelmina, let's go outside so you can get some of Daddy's delicious ribs!"

By the time Mama ran out of things for me to do, practically everybody had finished eating. Even Jazz was sitting on the grass without any food either in her mouth or on a plate in her lap.

I was picking up a platter of leftover food to take back into the kitchen when Mama stopped me. "Just leave that there," she said. She took the platter out of my hands. "Somebody might want to snack on this later. Besides, you've done more than your share!"

I wanted to tell Mama I was glad she had noticed, but I didn't. Then she leaned over and kissed me on the cheek and whispered, "I really appreciate all your help, Ernestine, and so does Marcus. He knows that he wouldn't have been able to spend time with Madelyn if you hadn't filled in for him today."

I shrugged my shoulders. Mama was making it hard to stay angry about having done so much work. But I had to say *something*. "Somebody had to do it, and it sure wasn't gonna be Jazz."

Mama laughed. "You're right about that. She didn't do her share of work, but she definitely ate her share of food." Mama looked at me before she kept talking. "Speaking of food, I haven't seen *you* eat anything. Here, baby, let me fix you a plate."

Mama reached for one of the paper plates on the table. I grabbed her hand. "No, Mama," I said. "That's okay."

"You've already eaten?" she said.

I figured it would be easier to tell a fib than to try to explain that I wasn't going to eat. Not for weeks. "Uh-huh," I said, "and I'm not hungry."

The second fib was worse than the first. While I was saying it, Daddy was pouring the last of his barbecue sauce on some ribs. When he saw me watching, he held up the tray of ribs and raised up his eyebrows in a way that meant "Want some?"

I shook my head to Daddy and told Mama I would see her later.

I looked around to see where Wilhelmina was. I couldn't find her for the longest time. Then I saw her standing with a bunch of the grown-ups.

I shoulda known. It's just like she does at school—always talkin' to the teachers insteada kids.

All of them were in a circle. Daddy, Uncle J. B., Mrs. Vines, and Gramma Taylor, Clovis's grandmother. And Wilhelmina. I was on my way over there to see what they were talking about when Wilhelmina saw me. She left them and came over to me.

"Ernestine!" she said, grabbing my arm. "Why didn't you tell me?"

"Tell you what?" I said. Wilhelmina's eyes were almost popping out of her head.

"About Monroe Street," she said.

"Oh, that."

"Whadda you mean, 'Oh, that'?" she said. I pulled my arm away to keep her from squeezing it any more.

"There's not much to tell," I said, "except about the river of glass."

"The *what?*" Wilhelmina's eyes got even bigger.

The look on her face made me laugh. "That's what people were sayin' about the glass all over the street. There was so much, it looked like a glass river. And it really did. I saw it when Uncle J. B. took me and Jazz over to Monroe Street the day after it happened."

Wilhelmina leaned down to get right in my face. Her voice got like it was almost whispering. "Your uncle J. B. was the one who said that it was white kids who did all the vandalism," she said.

"He *did?*" I could feel my eyes popping open as wide as Wilhelmina's had.

Wilhelmina straightened back up. "You didn't know?" she said.

The way she sounded and looked at me when she said that made me start getting angry. Plus, my stomach was growling so loud I almost couldn't stand it.

"I bet Uncle J. B. doesn't know for sure, either," I said.

I didn't know whether Uncle J. B. knew or didn't know. But I hadn't heard him say anything about it, and I figured I would have if he knew anything for sure.

I was about ready to tell Wilhelmina that I was going over

to talk to Uncle J. B. myself, and if she wanted to go with me she could. Then, just as I opened my mouth to speak, my stomach growled. Loud! So loud, it sounded like I had belched!

I slapped my hand over my mouth. At that exact minute I saw Billy Carson standing next to me. I could tell from the dumb grin on his face that he had heard the whole entire growl-belch.

"Hey, Ernestine," he said. "Amanda wants to know if there's any more ice."

I yanked the paper cup he was holding right out of his hand. But I didn't say that I would go into the kitchen to see. I just headed to the house so he'd know from watching me.

Now I'm a maid for Amanda Clay! Great!

12 ℘ *Amanda*

"Thanks, Billy."

I took the glass of ice and pop Billy was holding out to me. Out the corner of my eye, I could see Ernestine watching us. I gave Billy a big smile. Then I remembered how Madelyn tilts her head sometimes when she smiles at Marcus, and I did that, too.

"I'm glad you found some ice," I said.

Billy sort of hunched his shoulders. "I asked Ernestine for some," he said. "She got it from the kitchen."

I didn't know what else to say, so I just kept smiling. And Billy kept standing there.

This is sooooo weird!

I was trying to think of something to say when Billy kicked at the grass for the zillionth time. Then he said, "Uh,

I'm gonna go over and see if T-Bone wants to play some Ping-Pong. Wanna come?"

I was hoping everybody would start dancing like we had done the last time. The only thing people were doing so far was eating and standing and sitting around. And talking.

Maybe they'll put some music on later.

"Okay," I said.

The Ping-Pong table was set up near one of the big trees in the yard. I leaned against the tree to watch Billy and T-Bone play. I had done the same thing while I watched my dad and Marcus. They played a game before we started eating.

Dad and Marcus are terrific Ping-Pong players. Sometimes I can't believe how fast they can slap the ball around and not miss. Billy and T-Bone weren't anywhere *near* that good. They weren't terrible, but the game moved super slow.

I could tell that Billy was trying to show off. He did stuff like hit the ball really hard to make it bounce way up. Then he would say, "Yeah," like he had done something fantastic. Every now and then he would look over at me out the corner of his eye.

It was boring just standing there watching Billy and T-Bone. I was trying to decide what I could do when I heard the talking near the other side of the tree.

When I turned around, I saw Dad, my godmother, Ernestine's father and her uncle J. B., and two other women I didn't know. Most of them had been standing there talking a long time, but the group was getting bigger. And louder. Then I heard my dad above everybody.

"J. B.," he was saying, "you telling me it was kids from

over on Woodridge that did all that destruction on Monroe? A bunch of well-off white teenagers?"

"I'm not saying that's a fact. I'm saying that's one of the stories goin' around," Mr. J. B. said.

"Why would kids from Woodridge be on Monroe?" one of the ladies asked. "They don't live near there and there's nothing for them to do there…why would they be there at all?"

I had turned back around, acting like I was still watching the boring Ping-Pong game. I didn't want the grown-ups to know I was listening to them. But I leaned my head back as far as I could so I could hear everything.

"The word is that the Woodridge group has some kind of clubhouse over on Monroe. A place they go to get away from the overprotective eyes of their parents—"

Ernestine's dad had been talking when Godmother interrupted. "Excuse me, Ernest," she said, "but there's the same talk about some of the black kids who live near Monroe. That they have *their* own secret club down on Monroe."

A secret club on Monroe? I wonder who's in it?

I remembered the club I had started last year when we were in sixth grade. In my opinion it was a great club—the best one at Du Bois. After school ended, our C.L.U.B. just sort of stopped. Mostly because we all had summer stuff to do. Maybe we'd start it up again after school started. But I didn't want to think about that right then. I didn't want to miss anything they were saying. Not one word!

"You know," said another one of the women I didn't know, "Monroe's always been a mystery. Seems like white folks don't want nothin' to do with the street, but they don't want us to have it, either!"

Dad had been nodding his head. "It has the potential to be an economic oasis. Unfortunately it's stuck between the white and black communities. It seems destined to be a no-man's-land, I guess."

Suddenly, I remembered that my dad was saying one of the same things he had said one time when he dropped me off on Monroe for dance class.

I wish I had asked him what he meant.

This time I wanted *soooo* bad to ask that I almost couldn't keep my mouth closed. But I knew I had to. I wasn't even supposed to be listening.

"You're right about that, Clay," Mr. Harris said. It was weird to hear him call my dad by our last name. "The location makes Monroe an ideal street for business. Especially for the black community. But we just can't seem to get the money to make it happen."

"Maybe... just maybe something happened between the two groups," Godmother Frankie said. "You know, maybe the white kids and black kids got into it. The ones who have their clubs down there."

"That's what I'm beginning to think," J. B. said. "With all the desegregation issues..."

The what? What are they talkin' about?

It was getting harder to keep up with what they were saying. Especially with some of the words they were using. But I kept listening and standing there. Anyhow, the Ping-Pong game was still going on.

"My parents said that desegregation is going to be an issue all over the country."

I didn't know who said that, but I knew it was someone

who hadn't said anything until now. The voice sounded a little familiar.

"Your parents are absolutely right, Wilhelmina."

Wilhelmina? What's she doin' there?

I couldn't stop myself from turning around. When I did, I almost couldn't believe it. Wilhelmina was standing with all the grown-ups, talking like she knew as much as everybody else.

"They said the Supreme Court's decision about segregated schools being unlawful is going to change schools all over the country," she said. "Things will have to be...ah, fixed so black and white kids can go to the same schools."

All of the adults were sort of smiling at Wilhelmina while they listened to her. I knew she wasn't telling them anything they didn't already know. Their smiles were saying things like, "Isn't that Wilhelmina smart to know about stuff like we do."

"And I think that's why the white kids did all that vandalism on Monroe Street," Wilhelmina said. "Because they were mad about the new desegregation law."

"Hold on there, Wilhelmina," Ernestine's father said. He held up his hand like he wanted to stop Wilhelmina, even though the only thing that she moved had been her mouth.

"We don't know for a fact if it was white kids or not," Mr. Harris said. "No one knows *who* was responsible. And we should be extremely careful about spreading any rumors regarding a matter as sensitive as this."

So much for you, Miss Know-It-All!

Since Wilhelmina was standing there as big as anything,

I knew there was no reason for me not to be standing there with them, too. Especially since there was something I really wanted to find out. I walked over to where everybody was standing.

"I heard somebody over here say something about Monroe Street," I said. "Does anybody know what's gonna happen to the dance studio?"

Godmother Frankie gave me this big grin. "My godchild! The next Katherine Dunham!"

I tried not to smile, but I couldn't help myself.

"That's the good news in all of this," Mr. J. B. said. "Miss Davis's dance studio is already being fixed up. A bunch of us were over there this morning, cleanin' up the last of the glass, replacing the front windows, and doin' some other things to get the place in shape."

"That's right!"

This time the new voice came from Ernestine's mother. She and Ernestine had come over and were standing next to Ernestine's dad.

"The committee of mothers who've been getting the classes going are doing everything they can to make certain they stay that way!" Mrs. Harris said. "We're even hoping that getting the studio fixed up right away will help other good things happen on Monroe Street."

"When will the studio be fixed up, Mrs. Harris?" Wilhelmina wanted to know.

"Next week," Mrs. Harris said. "That's what we're aiming for."

"I hope so," Wilhelmina said, "because I'm anxious to start the classes."

"You're going to be taking the classes?" Mrs. Harris said. "That's wonderful, Wilhelmina!"

I didn't see what made it so wonderful. But I didn't say anything. Anyhow, Wilhelmina probably wouldn't last that long.

She's so tall! Too tall for a dancer, I think.

I was getting ready to ask Wilhelmina if she had taken dancing lessons where she had lived before, when I saw Ernestine watching me. She was standing between her mother and father, sort of grinning.

So, what are you grinnin' about?

I decided it was time to go back to see what Billy and T-Bone were doing. I looked over at Dad to smile at him before I left, but he had started talking to Mr. Harris. So I turned around without saying anything to anybody and went to the other side of the tree.

13 ✒ *Ernestine*

MISS DAVIS HELD UP her hand to get everybody to pay attention. "Okay, dancers," she said, "I want you to listen to this record very carefully. And I think it will help if you close your eyes while you listen. Closing your eyes will help you focus."

After she put on the record, Miss Davis sat on the floor like all the girls in the class were doing. Then she closed her eyes.

I was sitting at the piano. But I figured I might as well close my eyes like everybody else, so I did.

> *There is a balm in Gilead*
> *To make the wounded whole.*

I recognized the music right away. It was a song we sing at

my church all the time and one I like a lot. I had even played it for the choir to sing. It's a spiritual.

> *There is a balm in Gilead*
> *To heal the sin-sick soul.*

It seemed a little peculiar to be sitting on the piano bench with my eyes closed. But the more I listened, the more I stopped thinking about anything but the music.

> *Sometimes I feel discouraged,*
> *And think my work's in vain,*
> *But then the Holy Spirit*
> *Revives my soul again.*

The music to this song is slow. And the singing on the record was almost a kind of moaning. In a way you might expect the song to be sad, but it's really not. Miss Helen told me once at church that "There Is a Balm in Gilead" is a comforting song, just like the word "balm" means something to make you feel better.

Miss Helen was right.

I was thinking about the music so much that when it stopped I didn't open my eyes right away. After I did, I sneaked a look around to see if anybody had noticed me, still sitting there with my eyes shut. But it didn't look like anybody had.

Whew!

Miss Davis stood up. "I'm going to play that again," she said, "but before I do, let's talk about the music for a minute."

She started moving around the room. Not walking exactly. Not dancing either, but almost. Miss Davis is so graceful that whenever she moves it's close to dancing.

"How would you describe that music?" she said.

Nobody said anything, but some of the girls looked at each other. I saw Amanda look at Alicia and kind of hunch her shoulders. Then Alicia raised her hand.

"It's a spiritual," she said after Miss Davis called on her.

"Ah, so it is," Miss Davis said. She was still moving around the room. Sometimes walking between people. "That's one way to describe it. Is there anything you can tell about spirituals?"

I figured Wilhelmina was going to raise her hand. And I was right.

"Yes, Wilhelmina," Miss Davis said.

Wilhelmina stood up. She didn't have on the same dance outfit as everybody else because it was her first day in class. She had on a black leotard and tights. It made her look taller than ever. But she didn't look peculiar at all. She even looked like she was *supposed* to be a dancer.

Alicia had told me Amanda thought Wilhelmina was too tall to be a dancer. I looked over at Amanda to see if she was watching Wilhelmina. She was, but kind of sideways.

"Spirituals are folk songs," Wilhelmina said. "They were made up by the Africans brought to America to work as slaves. They were the songs they sang out in the fields."

"Thank you, Wilhelmina," Miss Davis said. I could tell from her voice and her smile that she was impressed. She even stopped moving around for a minute. I felt like telling her that a bunch of us in sixth grade had felt the same way the first time we heard Wilhelmina stand up and answer a question. That time she told Mrs. Williamson about W.E.B. Du Bois, Clarence White had looked at Wilhelmina looming over everybody and said she must be six feet of brains.

Wilhelmina's practically ten *feet of brains!*

Miss Davis started walking again. "Spirituals are a magnificent art form, born of our people," she said. "W.E.B. Du Bois has called them our 'sorrow songs.' This description of spirituals often comes to my mind when I listen to them. I find myself full of wonder, thinking how such beauty could come from so much pain."

It got so quiet in the room while she was talking I could almost hear people breathing.

Miss Davis went over to the record player again. "I'm going to play the same music again," she said. "I want you to listen carefully just as before, but this time with your eyes open. Because as I listen this time, I am going to express with my body how this song makes me feel."

> *There is a balm in Gilead*
> *To make the wounded whole.*
> *There is a balm in Gilead*
> *To heal the sin-sick soul.*

When the music started, Miss Davis closed her eyes and stretched out her arms. Very slowly. Then she started kind of pulling something from the air. Like she had found something she wanted to pour over her. While she was pouring, the expression on her face moved into a smile.

I could feel a smile coming on my face, and I didn't care if anybody was watching me or not. How Miss Davis was moving her body was amazing. It was beautiful!

> *Sometimes I feel discouraged*
> *And think my work's in vain,*
> *But then the Holy Spirit*
> *Revives my soul again.*

When the music changed, Miss Davis started bending over. Like she wanted to fold herself in two. Almost like something was hurting her. She stayed that way for a little while, swinging back and forth. Then she reached up with her whole body, raising her arms high above her head. It was almost like she was trying to reach far into the sky. She stood like that until the music stopped.

At first nobody made a sound. Then Alicia stood up and said, "Oh, Miss Davis, that was fantastic! I think I would have known how you were feeling even if I hadn't been listening to the music! I could tell that you were reaching for something to make you feel better—something like a balm, like the song says."

Alicia's voice sounded a little wobbly. I didn't look at her on purpose.

She's probably almost gettin' tears in her eyes like I am.

"What a lovely thing to say, Alicia," Miss Davis said. "And I'm certain I will feel the same way as I watch *you* express your response to the song." Miss Davis held out her arms and made a motion for everybody to stand up. "As I watch *all* of you use your bodies to paint a picture of how that music makes you feel."

For the first time since I had even heard about the dance classes, I wanted to be out there on the floor with everybody else. I *really* did. But I stayed where I was on the piano bench.

Miss Davis came over to the piano and put her arm around my shoulders. "Ernestine," she said. She was almost whispering. "Do you know this song?"

I nodded my head without looking at her. My eyes still felt kind of wobbly.

"Good," she said. "Play it for us." Then she patted me on my back. "And use your music to express your feelings just as we're going to use our bodies."

I nodded again.

"All right, class," Miss Davis said. "Instead of the record, Ernestine is going to play for us. This time as you listen, think only of how you feel. Focus your thoughts *inside* yourself and show on the outside how you feel."

I started playing the song. I knew it well enough to not have to look at the piano keys, so I thought about closing my eyes to see inside myself better. But I was afraid I might get *too* carried away.

I looked into the mirror instead. The new one they had put up was bigger than the one the vandals had wrecked. The new mirror covered the entire wall from one end of the room to the other.

The dancers really seemed to be trying hard to express how they felt. Even Edna who usually acts like she doesn't want to be bothered with anything. Wilhelmina stood out a lot, and not just because she's so tall. She was being kind of...dramatic.

Jazz is like that sometimes when she's showin' off.

Then I noticed Amanda. And when I did, I almost couldn't believe my eyes.

Amanda had closed her eyes like Miss Davis had done. Only you could tell that she wasn't trying to imitate the teacher. Instead of having her arms stretched out, Amanda had hers wrapped around herself.

For a while she stayed like that in one spot—holding herself while she kind of rocked her body. Every now and then she would drop her head back hard and roll it around.

Wow! She's actin' like she really has been wounded and is tryin' to put herself together again!

Watching Amanda made me feel something extra inside. I wanted to make what I was feeling show in the music. Keeping my eyes on Amanda helped me do that.

She started twirling. At first it was slow, then she started going faster. And then even faster! Her dance outfit whipped around so fast you could almost hear it!

Amanda started spinning out of the group and around the room. Her movements were so fast—and so good!—that the other girls stopped their own dancing to give her more room. They started watching *her*!

Near the last part of the song, Amanda stopped. It was all of a sudden, like she had heard someone yell, "Freeze!" After a little while she brought her arms up real slow and wrapped them around herself again. She dropped her head back again, but this time very slowly. Then she stood very, very still.

Amanda was amazing! She looked beautiful while she was dancin'!

All of a sudden, everybody started clapping and looking

at Amanda—and at me! I was surprised because I hadn't figured we were performing or anything even close. But hearing all the clapping *was* nice.

Then Miss Davis grabbed one of my hands and one of Amanda's hands and made us bow together. "You two make a great team," she said.

I took a bow and so did Amanda. But I didn't say one word, and neither did she.

14 □ *Amanda*

August 23, 1957

Dear Diary,

   Something really, really, REALLY weird happened at dance class yesterday. First Miss Davis played this music called "Balm in Gilead." After we listened to it, she showed us how the music made her feel. Then she told us to show her with our bodies how it made us feel.

   The music was soooo beautiful. But it was beautiful and sad, together. And all while I listened I couldn't think of anything else but how Dad and Mother are never going to live together with me again. Never. How we'll never be a whole family again. Not ever. And that's what I knew I had to express with my body like Miss Davis told us to.

   And you know what? I closed my eyes when I started

dancing, and after just a little while I forgot that there was anybody in the room but me. That sounds weird, doesn't it? But I did! I really, really forgot!!!! And you know I would never lie to you. Especially about this!

The song made me feel super sad when I started. I even thought I might get tears in my eyes, and that's one of the reasons I shut them. I also dropped my head back a few times to make sure I wouldn't get teary. Then—it was weird—the more I danced, the better I started feeling! I started feeling so much better, I didn't want to do anything but twirl and spin around the room. And I did it so much that by the time I stopped I actually felt like smiling!

It was... it was... I don't know how to describe how it was! Even the words "terrific" and "wonderful" and "fantastic" and "incredible" don't really tell how it was. But, Dear Diary, you'll find out for yourself because when Mother and I go shopping today for school shoes, I'm going to convince her to buy that record for me. Then I'll be able to play the music and dance to it anytime I want to. I'll be dancing just for you—and for me!

There's Mother, yelling for me to get ready.

Gotta go, but you and I know that A.W.R.T.W.D.F.!

Love,
ANC

P.S. This is a sort of a note to myself so I won't forget to tell you next time about what Ernestine and Wilhelmina did in class. It's good about E (can you believe

I'm saying that?) ~ she really IS a good piano player. But it's not good about W ~ she really ISN'T all that good a dancer. Alicia said she would be, but I knew she wouldn't be anything special.

One more time: Gotta go, but you and I know that A.W.R.T.W.D.F.!

Love again,
ANC

15 ✍ Ernestine

WHEN I WAS LITTLE and Mama had taken me to Miss Hattie's, I would bite on my tongue practically the whole time to keep from busting out laughing. Now I looked at Jazz and wondered if she was doing the same thing while she listened to Miss Hattie go on like she does.

Probably not. Jazz doesn't hold back anything!

I didn't know until later how right I had figured.

Miss Hattie has been fixing clothes for people in our neighborhood forever. She works as a seamstress at one of the fancy dress shops downtown. Mama calls Miss Hattie a tailor, which she says is much more than a seamstress.

"Anybody who can style and finish suits and coats like Hattie does is certainly a tailor," Mama said once. "And an accomplished one at that. If Hattie could afford to have her own shop she'd be rich!"

We always ended up at Miss Hattie's near the beginning of school, getting clothes hemmed or fixed. Usually Mama would sit on the little leather stool Miss Hattie's nephew brought her from Africa while I stood on the little platform Miss Hattie has in front of her long floor mirror. Mama would listen while Miss Hattie talked and talked. She would talk the whole entire time she was pinning the clothes to show how they needed to be fixed. And I would just stand there, trying to stay still, wishing Miss Hattie would please stop talking so much and hurry up.

Miss Hattie was going on worse than ever this time. I heard Daddy tell Mama once that Miss Hattie was an awful gossip. Mama told Daddy that in Miss Hattie's line of work, it's natural to hear a lot of news. Miss Hattie *did* seem to have something to say about practically everything—*and* everybody. I might not have been able to stand it if I hadn't had Jazz to look at while I stood there. It was almost funny to see Jazz watching Miss Hattie just like somebody watches a movie.

Usually Jazz doesn't come with us to Miss Hattie's. But this time Mama was having some of my old skirts cut down for Jazz. That meant Jazz was seeing the "Miss Hattie Show" for the first time, and she was practically staring down Miss Hattie's throat while she talked.

"And you know what I said? Umph! Mercy me! I said I didn't want nothin' to do with them folks outside of doin' what I got to do to make a livin'! That's what I said. Mercy me! I sure did!"

Even if you heard Miss Hattie talking in another room and didn't recognize her voice, you would still know who she was because of an expression she uses over and over while she talks. And it doesn't matter *what* she's talking about! The expression is "Mercy me" and she has been using it forever!

I think Miss Hattie was talking about some of the people she works for in the shop, but I didn't know for sure. I blocked out all the details and just heard the "Mercy me's" every now and then when they popped out.

"You know, Hattie," Mama said, "you really ought to figure out a way to have the customers come directly to you. You have to realize that one of the reasons the shop is so popular is because of your work."

"Mercy me, Louise! Don't you know I think about that all the time," Miss Hattie said. "Yes I do! Umph! Mercy me, I do!"

Miss Hattie held the straight pins in her mouth while she talked. She would pull them out one at a time to use. I figured she must have been holding them with her teeth because none ever fell out, no matter what she said.

"Them women in the shop would have conniption fits if I did that! Umph! Mercy me! Can't you just see that?"

Miss Hattie started laughing and shaking her head. "Mercy me!" she said about three times.

"So let them," Mother said. "They don't own you. They need you a lot more than you need them!"

The telephone rang just as Miss Hattie was putting the last pin in my dress. "Mercy me! Who is this callin' me this time of day?"

Miss Hattie got up from where she was kneeling by her little platform. "Umph! Y'all excuse me for a minute while I go see who this is." Miss Hattie even said "Mercy me" while she walked out of the room!

Mama got up and stood behind the platform. I was looking at myself in the mirror and could see her looking at me.

"Is the length okay?" Mama said.

I shrugged my shoulders. And I *know* Mama saw me because she was still looking at me.

"Well, is it?" she said again.

"I said it was okay," I said.

"No you didn't, Ernestine," Jazz butted in. "All you did was hunch your shoulders!"

I wanted to tell Jazz to mind her business when Mama said, "Jazz, this doesn't concern you."

Mama walked around to the side of the platform so she could look me right in the face. "What's the matter, Ernestine? Don't you like the dress anymore? Although I don't know why you shouldn't—you picked it out yourself. And in the store you said you liked it a lot."

Mama was going on the same way she had been doing all the time lately—asking questions and then answering them herself. I figured there wasn't anything left for me to say. So I just shrugged my shoulders again.

"Ernestine!" Mama was close to yelling.

I looked at her. I made sure my voice was low. "Yes?" I said.

Mama's eyes got kind of slitty. I could tell she was getting angry.

It's like she's just waiting for me to do something so she can yell at me.

"Yes, Mama?" I said.

Mama put her hands on her hips. "Ernestine, what is the

matter with you lately? It's like nothing suits you. First you say you like the dress, and now it's like you can't stand it—"

I cut Mama off—not to be a smart mouth, but because what she was saying wasn't true. "I didn't say nothin' about not likin' the dress. I didn't say nothin' at all!"

Mama's eyes were still slitty. "You don't have to say anything. Practically the whole time Hattie's been pinning up the dress you've been standing there, making faces at yourself."

"Mama, I wasn't—" I started.

Mama didn't let me finish. "And don't tell me you haven't been, Ernestine. I know you have because I've been watching you."

Since you know everything, I might as well sew my mouth shut!

I kept what I was thinking to myself and didn't even try to say anything else. But that didn't stop Mama. "Oh, you've been making the faces all right," she said.

Mama looked down at the floor and shook her head. When she looked back at me her eyes weren't slitty anymore and her voice was softer.

"Ernestine, is it the dress?" she asked me. "Or is it… Ernestine."

I jerked my head around so Mama couldn't see my face anymore. "What are you talkin' about?" I said. And I made *extra* sure to keep my voice low.

I felt Mama's hand on my arm. "I know about the diet, Ernestine," she said. "I know how you're trying to practically starve yourself so you'll lose some weight."

I was thinking about what I needed to say to get Mama straight, but she kept on talking.

"Baby, if you really want to lose weight, we should sit down and talk about it," Mama said, rubbing on my arm. "But not eating breakfast and hardly anything at dinner and then going to the kitchen in the middle of the night to get a sandwich is *not* the way to lose weight."

"I'm not trying to be on a diet! I'm not!" The words were out of my mouth almost before I knew it. And I was practically yelling. But I didn't care.

"Just because I don't like what we're havin' for breakfast or dinner doesn't mean I'm on some dumb diet," I said. "And anyway, everybody doesn't have to be some old skinny Minnie. I don't even want to be like that!"

I was almost afraid to look at Mama because I knew she was getting ready to bless me out good. I could feel my fingers balling up on both hands while I got myself ready to hear it.

But Mama didn't say anything. She just stood there, looking at me and not saying anything.

It felt like I was the one who needed to say something. I shouldn't have been yelling. Plus, Mama had been right.

In between listening and not listening to Miss Hattie, I *had* been looking at myself and making faces. I was noticing the ugly pimples all over my face. And how Miss Hattie's mirror made me look even bigger than Mama's. *And* how I wished I hadn't gotten *anything* new for school.

Not until I look good enough to fit into one of those dance outfits.

But I wasn't going to tell Mama that. I wasn't going to tell *anybody* that.

I'm just gonna stand here and wait for Mama to get her yellin' over with.

Then, before any of us could say anything, Miss Hattie came back into the room. She didn't just come in, she busted in!

"Oh, mercy me!" she said, walking over to Mama. "Louise, just wait until you hear! Oh, mercy, *mercy* me."

Miss Hattie's face was practically one enormous frown.

"Hattie, what's happened?" Mama said.

"That was your Ernest on the phone," Miss Hattie said.

"Ernest? Is something wrong with Ernest?" Mama reached out for Miss Hattie like she wanted to grab her. I understood exactly how she was feeling.

Oh no! Don't let something happen to Daddy. Please, PLEASE!

"What is it, Hattie? Tell me!" Mama was almost screaming at Miss Hattie.

"Ernest was calling to make sure you and the girls were over here with me and not down at that dance place on Monroe Street," Miss Hattie explained.

"What's happened on Monroe?" Mama said. She had put her hands on Miss Hattie's arms, but she wasn't almost screaming like she had been before.

"There's a fire," Miss Hattie said. "Mercy me, there's a big fire over on Monroe, and, mercy me, they think it's the dance place that's burning down!"

I was shocked. So was Mama. Both of us stood there not

knowing what to say. Jazz didn't know what to say either, but she said it anyway.

"Mercy me! That's awful! Umph! Mercy, mercy, *mercy* me!"

After Jazz let all those "mercies" out of her big mouth, there was nothing I could do to stop myself from laughing. I slapped my hand over my mouth to keep my laugh from showing and making noise, but it was too late. Even though I almost felt sorry for Jazz when I saw how Mama looked at her and knew how much trouble she was going to be in, I laughed. And I kept laughing even though Miss Hattie's ugly mirror was staring right in my face.

Then I remembered the horrible news Miss Hattie had told us before Jazz said anything, and I finally stopped.

16 ✎ Amanda

"DAD! YOU'RE FOOLIN', right?"

I could hardly believe what my dad was telling me. He just *had* to be fooling.

But Dad wouldn't joke about somethin' like this.

It was like Dad had read my mind. "Amanda," he said, "I wouldn't kid you about something like this. You know better than that."

"Yeah, I know," I said. But all I could think about was the stuff I *didn't* know.

"Dad, what happened? How did the fire start? Do you think somebody started it on purpose? You know, like they broke into the buildings and tore everything up? Who would *do* stuff like that?"

Dad flopped down in his chair. "You're asking the questions we *all* want the answers to, Amanda," he said.

"Can we drive over to Monroe Street to see what's happened? Please, Dad?"

"I'm sure it's a mess over there right now," he said. "The traffic will be terrible. There'll be fire trucks and police cars all over the place."

"Then, let's walk," I said. "It's not *that* far."

It was far enough, but I knew we could make it.

"No," Dad said, shaking his head. "Not now...not yet."

For the longest time, Dad just sat there in his favorite chair. It was the one that had been in our den at home. Except he had called it the library because that's where all his law books had been. The chair is the only furniture he took with him to his new house. It's old and sort of raggedy. I know that's why Mother didn't say anything about him moving it out. But Dad loves the chair like it was brand new.

Watching him just sit there, looking at the floor and not saying anything, was getting on my nerves. I wanted him to *do* something. Anything.

Then I thought of something *I* could do. "Excuse me, Dad," I said. "I gotta use the phone."

He still didn't say anything. But I knew he heard me because he nodded his head.

I went into Dad's bedroom to use the phone instead of using the one in the kitchen. I dialed the number and then sat on his bed while it rang. Mrs. Raymond answered.

"Hi, Mrs. Raymond, this is Amanda. Can I please speak to Alicia?"

"Hi, Amanda. She's right here."

"Hi, Amanda," Alicia said, coming on the phone right away.

"That was quick," I said. "You must have been sitting in your mom...your mom's lap."

I caught myself before I said "mommy." I was glad I had. Especially since Alicia hadn't even laughed about the lap part when she *knew* I had only been teasing. She didn't say anything.

"Alicia, are you still there?" I said.

"I'm here," she said. "Uh, did you call for something special?"

What's with her? She sure is actin' weird.

I was about ready to ask Alicia if something was wrong when she explained.

"I'm not trying to rush you or anything. It's just that my parents are getting ready to go visit my grandmother and Mommy's tellin' me and Edna some things she wants us to do while they're gone."

"Your parents are leaving you home by yourselves?" I couldn't believe it! Dr. Raymond's mother lives over a hundred miles away. Usually when they go to see her they stay overnight.

Alicia laughed. "I wish," she said. "Connie's gonna be here as usual. She'll be here after band practice. I told Mommy we didn't need a baby-sitter for just overnight, but she didn't listen."

She might if you stopped callin' her "Mommy."

I knew Alicia wouldn't think that was funny, either, so I didn't say anything.

"Amanda, can I call you back?" she said. "It won't be too long. They're gettin' ready to leave in a few minutes."

"Okay," I said, "but make sure you do because I want to tell you about the fire on Monroe Street. I think it's in the dance studio. And I'm at Dad's, okay? Bye!"

I started hanging up the phone, but I did it real slow. I wanted to see if Alicia was going to say anything else. If she hadn't already heard about the fire, I knew she was going to.

"The *what*? Fire? In our *studio*? Amanda? Amanda wait…"

That was all I heard before I hung up the phone. Then I laughed.

I bet she'll be callin' me back real soon!

The phone rang before I even finished stretching out on Dad's bed. I picked it up during the first ring so Dad wouldn't beat me to it.

"That was quick," I said again. "You must be building a nest on top of the phone." I just knew Alicia would laugh this time.

"Pardon me?"

It wasn't Alicia. It wasn't even a voice I had heard before. And it was a woman's voice.

Before I could decide what I should say, I heard myself saying "Huh?"

The voice laughed. Then it said, "May I speak to George, please?"

George?

Most of the time when Dad's clients call, they ask to speak to Attorney Clay. Hearing somebody who sounded like a stranger call him "George" was weird. I started to ask, "Do you mean Attorney Clay," but decided not to.

I yelled into the living room, "Dad! Phone." Then I

remembered Alicia and went to the bedroom door.

"Dad," I said, "Alicia said she was gonna call me right back. Do you think you'll be on the phone long?"

Dad just got up and walked to the phone. I stood at the bedroom door, waiting for him to answer me. He was looking at me when he picked up the phone.

"Hello?" he said.

As soon as Dad heard whoever it was on the other end, he turned around and faced the other way. But before he turned I saw him beginning to smile.

"Dad!"

Dad turned back around to look at me. He put his hand over the mouth part of the receiver before he said anything.

"What is it, Amanda?" he said.

"I wanna know if you're gonna be long," I said, "'cause Alicia said she was gonna call me right back."

"I won't be long," he said. Then he looked at me and smiled. "I'll call you when I'm finished, okay?"

"Okay," I said.

I stepped back into Dad's room, but I didn't close the door.

I heard Dad say, "My daughter." Then he said, "Yes, Amanda."

She knows me?

Then he said, "That's okay."

He didn't say anything for a long time. I wanted to peek around the door to see if he was still talking, but I was afraid he might see me and know I was listening.

I wonder if he's still smilin'?

I moved closer to the door to look through the crack where the door opens. I couldn't see anything, but I heard Dad say, "Ummmm. That sounds good. I love gumbo. Everybody from New Orleans loves gumbo."

Gumbo? Dad's talking about gumbo with one of his clients?

And then I knew. Dad *wasn't* talking to one of his clients. He was talking…he was talking to…

His girlfriend!

I almost couldn't think it. But as soon as I did, the thought kept running through my mind like it was a galloping horse.

The woman Dad's talkin' to is his girlfriend! He's tellin' her how much he loves gumbo because she's gonna fix him some gumbo. Just like that time Madelyn fixed Marcus some smothered chicken because he said he loved it.

I couldn't believe what I was thinking.

It can't be. It just can't!

Then Dad called me. "Amanda, I'm off the phone," he said.

I had been thinking so much I hadn't heard what else Dad had said. Was she coming over to fix him some gumbo? Was he going to where she lived? Where did she live? Who was she in the first place?

The questions were going in and out of my head so fast that I hadn't even seen Dad come in the bedroom.

"Amanda?" he said. "You look…ah, is anything wrong, sweetheart?"

I couldn't believe him! Didn't he know that I had just answered his phone and talked to his…his…his stupid girlfriend?

I couldn't stand it anymore! "Dad, I gotta go," I said.

Dad looked at me like *I* was the one doing something weird.

"What?" he said.

"I said, I gotta *go*!" I told him again. "I forgot about somethin' I have to do right away."

"I thought we were going to wait for a while and then go over to see what happened on Monroe Street," he said.

"It'll have to be later," I said. "I gotta get home right now. Before Alicia and her parents leave."

I was lying, but I didn't care.

I bet he's been lyin' to us plenty. He's never said one single word about his…

I had to make myself stop thinking about Dad and his… that woman. I snatched up the sweater I had brought with me in case it got cool later.

"I'll see you later, Dad," I said. I started to the front door.

"Amanda!" Dad almost shouted to make me stop. When he went on, his voice was softer. "Amanda, honey, wait. I'll drive you. I just have to put on my shoes, and that'll only take a few minutes. Just wait. Okay?"

I nodded my head. But when Dad turned to go back into his bedroom, I headed straight for the door. I only stopped for one second to kick his raggedy old chair.

I closed the door as soft as I could, and when I got outside, I started running.

Maybe runnin' does the same thing spinnin' and twirlin' do when you dance. Maybe it can make you feel better.

I ran as fast as I could.

17 ✎ *Ernestine*

MAMA AND JAZZ and me left Miss Hattie's to go home right after Miss Hattie told us about the fire. Mama said she would bring Jazz back later to get the rest of the fitting done. Then Mama rushed down the street like Miss Hattie had told her the fire was in *our* house.

Mama didn't stop until she got on our front walk and saw Daddy standing at the front door. "Oh, Ernest," she said. She put her hand on her chest. "I just had to get here. I was so afraid that..."

Daddy came out and met us on the porch. "I figured you'd start worrying," he said. He put his arms around Mama. "That's why I told Hattie to be sure to tell you why I had called."

"She did, she did," Mama said. "It's just that when you hear the word fire, you don't know *what* to think."

That's when Mama remembered what Jazz had said when *she* heard the word fire.

"And *you*, young lady," Mama said, pointing her finger at Jazz, "are in a *world* of trouble!" Mama looked at Daddy. "Just wait until you hear what your daughter did," she said.

Jazz looked like she wanted to disappear. For once she didn't have anything to say. But I could tell she was thinking about it and would come up with something soon.

I figured this would be a good time for me to find out for myself what had happened on Monroe Street.

If I ask Mama if I can go over there she'll say "no." But if I just say I'm gonna go over to Wilhelmina's...

"Mama, I'm goin' over to Wilhelmina's and tell her what's happened," I said. "Okay?"

"Fine, Ernestine," Mama said. "Don't be too long."

I started to make a face at Jazz before I left. Then I changed my mind.

She already feels bad enough, and when Mama gets through, she's gonna feel worse.

On my way down the street I felt in my pocket to see if I had a dime I could use to buy a candy bar or something for Jazz on my way back home.

Jackson Street is kind of divided into two parts. The part closest to my house has mostly stores; the Jackson Street Cafe is in that part. The other part has mostly houses and is where Wilhelmina's aunt lives. Practically the whole time I walked through the store part to get to Wilhelmina's, I heard people talking about the fire.

"They're saying some kids started it," said a lady standing in front of the beauty parlor. "And I bet you money it was those same kids who did all that other stuff over there on Monroe!"

A man parked in front of the Jackson Street Cafe was saying practically the same thing. "It *had* to be kids," he said. "Who else is gonna be that stupid? Who else would set a fire in a building that's almost empty? It *had* to be somebody stupid!"

You're the one who's stupid! Just because somebody's a kid doesn't mean they set fires. And it sure doesn't mean they're stupid!

I wanted to yell what I was thinking so bad, I had to bite the insides of my cheeks to keep from saying it out loud. I was still doing that when I heard somebody calling my name.

"Ernestine!"

I turned around and saw Wilhelmina. She was coming down the street behind me.

"Where'd you come from?" I said. "I was on my way to your house."

"Girl, have you heard about the fire?" she said.

"That's what I was comin' to tell you about," I said.

Wilhelmina grabbed my arm to pull me with her across the street.

"Where you goin'?" I said. "Your house is over there." I pointed to her aunt's house. It was a little farther down on the side of the street we were leaving.

"I *know* where I live, Ernestine," Wilhelmina said.

I think right after she heard herself she realized how it sounded. She gave me one of her half smiles. "I don't want Aunt Leola to stop us," she said.

"Stop us from what?"

"From going over to Monroe Street," Wilhelmina said. "Don't you want to find out for yourself what happened?"

"The only thing we gonna find out over there is what building caught on fire," I said. "And I already know that. It's the one where the dance studio is."

"But you don't know what *happened*," Wilhelmina said.

"You don't, either!" I said. I could feel my eyes getting a little slitty.

Wilhelmina gave me another one of her half smiles. "But I have a pretty good idea," she said. Then she turned around and started back down the street.

You always thinkin' you have a good idea about somethin'!

The words were ready to pop out of my mouth when I remembered what had happened the last time I had said practically the same exact thing to Wilhelmina.

It was just before she had left for the summer to visit her parents. I had come over to her house to bring the cookies Mama had baked for her to take on the train.

"Ummm. Oatmeal-raisin with nuts," Wilhelmina had said, looking in the cookie tin. "With these and everything Aunt Leola is fixing for me, I'm going to have a feast on the train."

"Is it scary taking a train by yourself?" I said. I was probably thinking about myself more than Wilhelmina. Nothing seemed to scare her.

"Not really," she said, shrugging her shoulders. "It's more boring than anything."

Wilhelmina held out the tin to offer me a cookie. I thought about the four I had snatched before Mama packed the tin, and said, "No, thanks."

Wilhelmina bit into one of the cookies. "But when I'm almost ready to scream from boredom, I think about my parents and how much they'll have to tell me when I get there."

"Like what?" I said.

"Like how much my father enjoys teaching at the university in Greensboro and how much progress they're making on the house they're building and—"

"Your parents are buildin' a house? You never said anything about that!"

Wilhelmina was holding the cookie in front of her face like a fan. She looked at me over the top of the cookie, but she didn't say anything.

"Will you be moving there when the house is finished?" I asked her.

"Of course!" Wilhelmina said. "Why wouldn't I?" She took another bite of the cookie. "The house is the main reason I haven't moved to North Carolina yet. But I have a pretty good idea that I'll be moving there soon. Maybe even in time to go to school there."

Wilhelmina took another bite of her cookie. "Ummm," she said. "Yep, a pretty good idea."

I was getting ready to ask how come she thought so. But even though Wilhelmina was chewing on her cookie and making sounds like everything was delicious, her eyes looked sad. *Really* sad. Almost like she might be ready to cry.

Her look was what I remembered while I followed Wilhelmina up Jackson Street.

If I say something about her always havin' a good idea about stuff, she might remember that, too.

I decided not to say anything. I just started walking again.

Just before we got to the end of Jackson, Wilhelmina turned into the alley. It's a shortcut to Fourth Street which is the best way to get to Monroe. But when I saw where she was headed, I started hearing Mama's voice in my head.

"Ernestine, don't ever let me catch you walking through an alley," her voice was saying. "Alleys are filled with hidden dangers."

Just this once, Mama.

I started running to keep myself from thinking. After a while I even passed Wilhelmina whose long legs move so fast, it's like she's running practically all the time.

We started smelling smoke while we were still on Fourth Street. By the time we turned the last corner and got to Monroe, the smell was awful. But it wasn't anywhere near as awful as what we saw.

The building where the dance studio had been was only half there. Not even half. It was almost like a skeleton of a building, but not the whole skeleton. Seeing it made me think of the skeleton in Dr. Redd's office where Mama takes us to get checkups. Dr. Redd calls his skeleton C. T. He always asks kids who come there to tell him what parts we think C. T. is missing.

That's what I started doing while I stood there, looking

at the used-to-be building. I tried to figure out what was missing.

The roof. Almost all of the wall on the left side. All the windows and doors. Miss Davis's sign.

I turned my head away. I wanted to shake out the picture I was getting in my mind. The picture of the new sign Miss Davis had put up when the studio had been ready the second time. The new sign had red letters instead of black ones like the first one had. The same thing had been written on both signs, but the new sign had pictures of dancers painted on both ends.

And now all the dancers have burned up.

I heard Wilhelmina's voice, but it sounded far away. "What did you say?" I asked her. Then I looked at her for the first time since we had been on Monroe Street.

Wilhelmina's face looked like practically everything on it was pinched. Her eyes were real narrow, her cheeks were sucked in, and her mouth had almost disappeared. Only her nose was the same. But wider than usual. The way noses can look when you're breathing heavy and not using your mouth to help.

She looked scary.

"Wilhelmina," I said, "are you okay?"

She didn't say anything for a long time. And her face stayed pinched.

"Wilhelmina," I said again. "Is anything wrong?"

"Is anything *wrong?*" Wilhelmina said, only she hissed it more than she said it. Then she looked at me. "*Everything's* wrong, Ernestine. Can't you see that?"

"I was talkin' about *you*, Wilhelmina," I said.

There she goes again!

"I can *see* what's wrong here," I said. I hoped my voice sounded as mad as I felt. "I was just askin' because you look so...so peculiar."

"I guess that's because I *feel* peculiar," she said. "I feel *extremely* peculiar, don't you?"

I didn't say anything. I figured it wouldn't make any difference whether I did or not. And it didn't.

Wilhelmina kept talking. "Doesn't it make you feel *peculiar* to know that a bunch of white kids burned down your dance studio?" she said.

What's she talkin' about?

What I was thinking must have shown on my face.

"That's who did it, you know," Wilhelmina said. "The same kids as before."

"How do you know?" I said.

"Who else?" she said. The more she talked, the louder her voice was getting. "Who else wants to make sure we don't have anything for ourselves? We can't go to their stupid segregated Marvelous Park or sit where we want in their smelly movie theater. And we *sure* can't take dance classes over on Merritt Avenue!"

Wilhelmina spit before she said the last thing. "And now we can't even have our *own* dance studio."

I still wanted to know how Wilhelmina had found all this out. "Wilhelmina," I started, "how do—"

"Don't ask me again how I know, Ernestine," she said, cutting me off. And this time she really did yell. "I JUST DO!"

Without saying anything else, Wilhelmina turned around and started running down the street.

While I watched Wilhelmina, I felt like I had been divided into two parts. Just like Jackson Street. Part of me wanted to run after her and make her tell me everything she knew about what had been happening on Monroe Street. The other part kept me knowing how angry Wilhelmina had made me. And *that* part kept my feet from moving one inch.

18 ✄ *Amanda*

AFTER I LEFT my dad's, I ran for four blocks without stop-ping. At the first corner, I got off Lendall, where Dad lives. I knew he was going to come after me, and I didn't want him to find me.

Let him wonder about me for a change, just like I wonder about him and his...

By the time I got to Grant, I had stopped running. But I walked fast. Grant is a crummy street. And I kept checking behind me to make sure Dad wasn't anywhere in sight.

I wondered if Dad would call Mother to tell her how I had run off without saying anything. I knew Mother would have a fit if he did—and I knew *he* knew she would, too.

I wish he couldn't ever find me. That would teach him.

I was concentrating so hard on all the things that I might be able to do to pay Dad back for what he was doing to us, that when I saw the street sign saying "Monroe" I almost couldn't believe it.

I've gone fourteen blocks!

Then I saw the fire trucks and police cars. And I remembered.

Our dance studio. It's gone.

I couldn't decide whether to keep walking down Monroe Street or stay on the corner where I was. When I was at my dad's, I had wanted to see what had happened. But standing there, looking at all the mess in the street, I wasn't sure if I did or not.

I was still deciding when I saw Ernestine and Wilhelmina. They were standing right across from the burned-down building. It looked like Wilhelmina was doing most of the talking.

As usual. She's such a know-it-all.

From the way Wilhelmina was pointing at the building and using her hands while she talked, I could tell that she probably knew something about what had happened. That's what made me decide to keep walking down Monroe. Then before I got to where they were, Wilhelmina turned the other way and started running down the street.

Oh well, Ernestine'll tell me.

I started running to get to Ernestine before she decided to take off down the street, too. It didn't look like she was going to move, but I yelled to her anyhow.

"Hey, Ernestine! Wait up!" I said.

When Ernestine turned around to see who was calling her, she looked sort of mad. But she sounded okay when she spoke.

"Oh, hi, Amanda," she said. "I didn't see you."

"I guess not. You were so busy listenin' to Wilhelmina. What was she tellin' you, anyhow? Did you find out anything new?"

"Whadda you mean? New about what?"

I couldn't believe her! There we were, standing in front of our burned-down dance studio that somebody had tried to break up with bricks only a couple of weeks ago, and Ernestine was asking me what did I mean.

I knew that if I told her how weird she was acting, I wouldn't find out anything. So I didn't say anything and just kept speaking in my normal voice.

"About Monroe Street, Ernestine," I said. "You know, everything that's been happening down here." I smiled at her. "What else would I be talkin' about?" I asked.

Ernestine shrugged her shoulders. "How would I know?" she said. "I can't read your mind."

"Nobody's askin' you to, Ernestine," I said, talking as nice as I could. "All I asked was did Wilhelmina tell you anything about what's been happenin' here on Monroe Street."

"That's not what you asked me, Amanda. You said—"

I just couldn't stop myself from cutting her off. She was really beginning to get on my nerves. "Ernestine, I *know* what I said. *You* know what I meant."

Ernestine put her hands on her hips and got right in my face. "You oughta say what you mean, Amanda," she said, "then I wouldn't have to try to read your mind."

"What's all this 'read your mind' mess?" I said, getting right back in her face. "How come you can't just answer my question?"

"Maybe 'cause you didn't *ask* your question. What you asked was—"

"Forget it, Ernestine!" I said. I had cut her off again, but I couldn't help it. "Just forget it!" I was ready to turn around and go back down the street.

"Forget what?" She started looking at me like *I* had a problem. "You haven't said anything for me to forget, Amanda!"

I wanted to tell her off good! "You know somethin', Ernestine," I said, "what I think is—"

Then she cut *me* off. "I *know* plenty, Amanda, but like I said, since I can't read your mind, one thing I *don't* know is what you think."

"Well, here's one thing you *can* know, Ernestine Harris," I said. "All I was doin' in the first place was askin' you a simple question. And I asked it nice! You're the one who started makin' somethin' out of it."

"I'm not makin' nothin' out of anything!" she said. "How come you always accusing me of junk?"

She was making me so mad I could feel my cheeks getting hot. "I didn't accuse you of anything!" I said. "All I asked was did you hear anything new about what's been happening on Monroe Street. That's *all* I said."

She *still* didn't stop! "Amanda," she said, "that's *not* what you said. If you had said that, I woulda known how to answer instead of havin' to ask you what you were talkin' about."

Suddenly it looked like Ernestine was beginning to smile. It was really weird. But seeing her face look that way made me stop being so angry.

"Ernestine," I said, "why do you always make it so hard to talk to you?"

"*I'm* not the one who makes it hard, Amanda. It's you!" she said.

"It is *not* me!" I said back. "All I said was—"

"Are we gonna go over that *again?* Look, Amanda—"

"No, *you* look, Ernestine. And you need to *listen*, too…"

But before I could say anything else, Ernestine started laughing. I couldn't believe it. First she had been trying to bite my head off, and now she was laughing. It made me start laughing, too.

It was too weird to be happening. There we were, me and Ernestine Harris, standing in front of our dance studio that had been burned to the ground, and almost laughing our heads off.

Finally we stopped. Then Ernestine looked at me. "Listen, Amanda," she said, "I did kinda know what you were askin'. I just didn't feel like…"

She sort of mumbled. I didn't say anything and waited for her to keep on.

"Wilhelmina was tellin' me stuff about Monroe Street," she said. "About how it's been a bunch of white kids who've been doin' all the stuff and—"

I didn't want to cut her off again, but I had to. Wilhelmina was still trying to be a know-it-all. She was saying the same thing she had said at the cookout. And the grown-ups had told her then she shouldn't be saying that.

"Ernestine," I said, "Wilhelmina doesn't know what she's talkin' about. Nobody knows whether that stuff about white kids is true or not. Even your *dad* said that to Wilhelmina and told her she needed to stop spreading rumors."

For the longest time, Ernestine just stood there, staring at me. It was like she was trying to decide whether *I* was telling the truth or not. And seeing her look at me like that began to make *me* mad.

"Listen," I said, "I don't care what you think. All I know is—"

Ernestine didn't let me finish. "All *you* know is the same thing everybody else knows, which is that *nobody* knows nothin' about what really happened!" she said. "And that includes Wilhelmina!"

Ernestine's face started getting puffed up, and her eyes got narrow like she was squinting. "And *you* don't need to be spreadin' no rumors about what *Wilhelmina* said either," she said, " 'cause all she's sayin' is that it sure coulda been white kids doin' all this stuff because of all the other rotten stuff they been doin' to us for practically forever!"

"Look Ernestine," I started, "all I said was Wilhelmina needs to—"

"Amanda," Ernestine said, cutting me off again, "if you have stuff to tell Wilhelmina, you need to tell her yourself!"

Ernestine was back up in my face. I felt like slapping her! That's when I heard someone yelling at me.

"Amanda!"

It was Dad. He was walking down the street to where Ernestine and I were standing.

Dad's gonna start yellin' at me in front of Ernestine!

I couldn't think of anything to say, or do. I just stood there, watching Dad march down the street.

He started in as soon as he got close enough to talk.

"Amanda, I've been looking for you *everywhere*! I don't know what possessed you to run out *or* to come here. But if you ever, again…" Dad's voice sort of drifted off before he went on.

"I don't know what either of you young ladies is doing here," he said. "I *know* one of you is here without permission, and I strongly suspect that the other is as well!"

Ernestine's in trouble, too? Did she run off from one of her parents?

I didn't say anything. Neither did Ernestine.

"I suggest that you both proceed to my car," Dad said.

I looked at Dad's face. He was really mad!

"Dad…" I started, but he didn't let me finish.

"Let me put that another way," Dad said. "That's not a suggestion. It's an order, and one I think you should carry out posthaste!"

I thought about asking Dad what "posthaste" meant, but decided that wouldn't be a good idea. I just started walking.

Ernestine decided the same thing. We also both decided not to say anything else to each other, even after we got in the car and Dad started driving us home.

19 ❧ *Ernestine*

"ERNESTINE, PLEASE?"

Jazz was right in my face, trying as hard as she could to look pitiful. But all she looked was dumb. Jazz can't look pitiful even when she tries.

"Ernestine, please, *pleeeeeease* tell Mama you wanna walk over to Monroe Street. Mama won't let me go myself, and I gotta see how everything looks over there now, and the only way I'm gonna get to see is if—"

"Look, Jazz," I said, cutting her off. "I already told you I have to write to Clovis."

"You *all* the time writin' to Clovis," Jazz said, kind of whining.

"That's 'cause I '*all* the time' have something to tell him," I said in the same fake pitiful voice she was using.

I sat down at the desk that's between my bed and Jazz's

and took out a couple of sheets from my box of stationery. I figured if I didn't say anything else and just started writing my letter, she'd leave me alone.

I figured wrong. Jazz sat down on her bed, put her elbows on the desk and started staring at me. Even though I wasn't looking right at her, I could see what she was doing out the corner of my eye.

I ignored her and started writing my letter.

September 1, 1957

Dear Clovis,
There is a GIANT pest in the room with me now, but I have so much to tell you that I can't wait for this GIANT pest to leave before I start my letter. So if you see a lot of spelling mistakes, it's not really my fault. It's because this GIANT pest is hanging around and won't get lost.

I hoped Jazz was trying to read what I was writing like she usually does. In case she was, I added one more thing.

Clovis, you are <u>extremely</u> lucky not to have ANY sisters. All they do is try to drive you crazy!

I looked over at Jazz. She was still plunked there on the desk, staring at my face.

"Jazz, I *told* you I'm gonna write my letter, so you might as well go on and leave me alone," I said.

"I'm not botherin' you," she said. "I haven't said nothin'

or touched you or anything. And this is my desk, too, so I have just as much right to be here as you."

I could tell from the way she sounded that Jazz wasn't ready to give up, and that the only thing I could do was keep on ignoring her. So I did.

Tomorrow is Labor Day. That means our summer is officially gone and that school will be starting. The only good thing is being in seventh grade. We get one more day—eighth graders too. School doesn't start for us until Wednesday. All the other grades at Du Bois start on Tuesday.

I was waiting for Jazz to get tired of being such a pain and to leave before I wrote the important part of my letter. Out the corner of my eye I could tell she had stopped staring at me and was looking out the window. I figured I wouldn't have to wait too much longer.

Marcus left yesterday to go back to college. Remember how I told you a few letters ago about the junky car he bought? Well, after he got it all packed with his stuff, the car kind of sagged in the middle. We all laughed when Marcus backed out of the driveway and started down the street. In a way that was good, though. If I hadn't been laughing I might have started to cry, and I think Mama felt the same way. We're both going to miss Marcus like crazy!

Jazz stopped leaning on the desk, but she didn't get up like I thought she was going to. She just rested on her pillow

MYSTERIES ON MONROE STREET

and went back to staring at me. Only this time it was more like glaring.

I had to try one more time to get rid of her. "I'm gonna remember this, Jazz," I said, "and the next time you really, *really* want me to do something, I'm not even gonna listen because you're being such a giant, *enormous* PAIN!" I glared back at her.

Jazz turned her nose up at me. "I'm not doin' nothin' to you, Ernestine Harris," she said. "All I'm doin' is bein' in here which is my room just as much as it's yours and mindin' my business. I'm not even makin' any noise and..."

I stopped listening. It was hopeless. All I could do was turn my back to her as much as I could so she couldn't see what I was writing without getting up and looking over my shoulder. It was the only thing I could do. I had to keep writing so I could get to the news I knew Clovis was dying to hear.

In your last letter you said you couldn't wait to find out more about the fire on Monroe. Actually I couldn't wait to tell you, but I didn't find out until yesterday. Now I can. The mystery has been solved!!!!

I drew a picture of a little horn. Clovis would probably figure out what it meant, but to make sure I wrote "Ta dah" in little letters above the picture and drew in some sound lines.

The man who owned the building set it on fire! Isn't that crazy? Daddy said the man burned the building down so he could collect the insurance he had on the building. I don't know how that works, but Daddy and Uncle J. B. were saying how the insurance was worth more than the building. Isn't that peculiar? Anyhow, the man confessed—and that's exactly what Uncle J. B. called it. Listening to Uncle J. B. talk about the fire was almost like hearing one of those mystery shows they used to have on the radio!

I remembered how all of us had been outside, packing up Marcus's car and listening and Daddy and Uncle J. B. talk about the fire. It had been kind of exciting to hear the details, but kind of scary too. And a little sad.

Daddy said the man might have done all the other wrecking on Monroe Street. The man <u>didn't</u> confess about that, though. Mama said we might never find out who did that. Wilhelmina still thinks it was the white kids who had that club on Monroe Street. She says they're mad about all the integration stuff.

Are they talking about that in Georgia—you know, about black and white kids going to school together? Will you be going to school with white kids? Mama and Daddy were explaining to me and Jazz that people here are going to be figuring out how to integrate the schools in Carey for next year, but that this year we're going to stay where we are. To me, that's what the BIG mystery is—all this talk about integration. It can really get confusing. I don't want to go to a school just to be around white kids. That's dumb. But the school they have for the white kids <u>is</u> better. A lot better. And that's what's <u>really</u> dumb!

When I talked to Mama about the jumble of feelings I had about everything that happened on Monroe Street, she said it was normal having mixed feelings about something so complicated. She said it meant I was growing up. I'm not sure I understand how that works, but Mama made it sound like it was something good, so it must be okay.

Clovis there's...

Before I wrote any more, I turned around to see what Jazz was doing. It had gotten so quiet, I thought she may have fallen asleep. She wasn't, but at least she wasn't still sitting there glaring. She didn't say anything when she saw me looking at her, and I didn't say anything either.

...one more thing I have to tell you. And I would only tell this to a BEST friend. So, you know what that means. You can't even tell this to your cat. Okay? Okay!

I looked around one more time to make doubly sure Jazz wasn't stretching her neck to see over my shoulder. Then I kept writing.

Before he left Marcus told me how he knew about my diet. He said he had been noticing me in Mama's room a lot, looking at myself in her mirror. He said people should take a long look at themselves, but that it was important to do it with an attitude. Marcus said my attitude for looking at myself was lousy, and that if I don't look at myself in a positive way, nobody else will. I'm pretty sure I understand what he means, but I'm not sure I know how to do it.

Suddenly, I started missing Clovis like crazy. It was *very* peculiar. There I was, right in the middle of a conversation with him—because that's what writing a letter is like—and missing him all at the same time.

I wanted to tell Clovis how hard it was to keep looking at myself in a positive way when I saw something so negative whenever I looked into a mirror. I had wanted to say the same thing to Marcus. But I was afraid that if I said something like that, it would sound like I was trying to make excuses for eating so much.

Maybe I'll never be thin. Maybe I should get used to looking the way I do.

Thinking about what Marcus had said and trying to figure out a way to explain it to Clovis started to get me down.

How can I tell Clovis how I'm feelin' when I don't even know myself?

I decided to just end the letter.

That's all for now. I'll write again Wednesday, as soon as I get home from school. I know you'll want to know everything, and IF I'm in a good mood, I'll tell you. (Just kidding. You know I will.)
Bye!

Love,
Ernestine

After I folded the letter and put it in an envelope, I looked at Jazz again. She was still there, resting against her pillow, and not doing or saying anything.

"Jazz, you feeling okay?" I asked.

"Uh huh," she said.

"Then why are you sittin' there like a lump?"

" 'Cause the only thing I *really* want to do is walk over to Monroe Street, and I want you to walk with me."

She said it plain—no whining, no pouting, no trying to be pitiful. Just regular. Like she was telling the complete truth.

Maybe that's what got me. "Okay, Jazz," I said. "We'll walk over there, and I'll mail my letter on the way."

Jazz jumped up from the bed like I had given her money. She threw her arms around me and gave me a big hug. In a way it was peculiar, but in another way it wasn't.

I guess I'm gonna have to get used to having a whole bunch of these growing-up times.

20 🙠 Amanda

"MADELYN? Can I come in?"

I knew Madelyn was in her room because I could hear her sniffling. I knocked again.

"Madelyn?" I waited to see if she was going to answer before I said, "I know you're feelin' bad, Madelyn, and I'm not comin' in to get on your nerves. I just wanna talk."

It sounded like the sniffling stopped. I opened the door a crack and peeked in.

Madelyn was sitting on her bed. She wasn't crying, but I knew she had been. I could tell her eyes were red even though she was looking at the wall in front of her and not at me. And there were balled up tissues on the floor. Marcus's picture was in her lap.

I bet she was clutchin' that picture like it was Marcus and just now put it down when she heard me comin' in.

I didn't tell Madelyn what I was thinking because I really *didn't* want to get on her nerves.

"Madelyn, can I ask you something?" I said.

She kept looking at the wall.

"Madelyn?" I said again.

Finally she turned her head and looked at me. "What do you want, Amanda?" she said.

I sat on the bed next to her and waited for her to tell me to move. When she didn't, I made myself comfortable.

"I'm sorry you're feelin' bad," I said. And I was. "I wish Marcus was still here, too." And I did. Marcus is the coolest member of the Harris family.

Madelyn smiled. But she wiped at her eyes with a tissue at the same time.

For a minute or two we just sat there, not saying anything. I wanted to give Madelyn time to finish crying again, in case she was.

"What did you want to ask me?" Madelyn said.

"I was just wonderin'…" I said, and then stopped. I was getting ready to ask Madelyn about Dad. Whether she knew about his…his friend who was a woman. But if I started off asking Madelyn about that, I knew she'd feel even more terrible. Especially if she didn't already know and I was telling her for the first time. So I decided to ask her about something else first.

"I was wonderin' if you knew anything about the fire and other stuff on Monroe Street," I said. "I heard you and Marcus talkin' about it the last time he was here."

Madelyn didn't say anything, but she nodded her head. So I kept talking. "What did Marcus mean about the mess on Monroe Street bein' only the beginning?"

Madelyn got up and walked over to the window. She took Marcus's picture with her.

"Are there gonna be more fires?" I asked.

"That's not what he meant," she said. "The fire on Monroe was started by somebody greedy and dishonest. But the vandalism might have been done by somebody or a group trying to make a point."

"Make a point?" I wanted to tell Madelyn she wasn't making sense, but I decided to wait.

She started looking out the window. "Things are changing, Amanda," she said. "The new law about integrating schools is just the beginning. There's going to have to be a lot of other changes, too. That's what Marcus was talking about."

Madelyn was still looking out the window, but she started clutching Marcus's picture against her chest. I don't think she even realized what she was doing.

"What kind of changes?" I asked.

"Changes to make things right," she said. She turned around to look at me, but she was still clutching her picture.

"Like being able to sit anywhere we want to when we go to the movie theater," she said.

"You don't go to the movies anymore," I said. And she didn't. Not since she started going with Marcus.

"That's why," Madelyn said. "And I'm not *going* to until I can sit anywhere I want."

I started to say I thought the best seats were always going to be in the balcony where you didn't have to worry about somebody's head getting in the way, but I knew that would tick Madelyn off.

Hearing her talk about sitting anywhere she wanted made me remember something. "Now black people can sit anywhere we want when we get on the bus," I said. "It used to be that we could only sit in the back. Then one day that just stopped."

Madelyn laughed. Anyhow, that's what it sort of sounded like. But from her face, it didn't look like she thought what I had said was funny at all.

"Having to sit in the back of the buses didn't just *stop*, Amanda," she said. She sounded like Dad the way he talks to me sometimes when he thinks I don't do anything in school but have recess. And that sound *really* gets on my nerves.

"So, how did it happen?" I said.

Madelyn looked at me and then she gave one of her super long breaths.

"I'm sorry, Amanda," she said. "You're growing up so much that sometimes I forget you're only twelve."

She did another long breath. "Let's talk about this another time, and then I'll tell you all about the bus boycott in Montgomery, Alabama, and about Martin Luther King—"

I cut Madelyn off. "For your information, I know about him," I said. And I did. And after I heard her say Montgomery, Alabama, I knew I had heard something about that, too, but I wasn't going to tell her that until I remembered what it was.

Madelyn smiled. It was a real smile. "I'm sure you know much more than we give you credit for, Amanda," she said. "But can we talk about this later? Please?"

"Okay, Madelyn," I said, "but I do have one really,

really, *really* important last thing to ask you—"

While I was talking, Madelyn closed her eyes. That's when I saw the tears on her cheeks. And she was hanging on to that picture like it was going to save her life.

She really is feelin' terrible about Marcus leavin'.

That's when I decided I couldn't say anything about Dad right then. I'd have to wait until later.

"Okay, Amanda," she said. "One last question."

"Uh," I said, "what point was somebody trying to make over on Monroe Street?"

I really didn't care about that right then, but it was the only question I could think of to put in the place of the one I decided not to ask about.

"I really don't know, Amanda," she said. "Maybe it was just some kind of sick protest."

"Some kind of what?"

"Protest. You know, something people do to let others know they don't like what's going on. Doing something destructive makes the protest sick." Madelyn shook her head. "But maybe it wasn't a protest. I just don't know," she said.

I got up from her bed. "Well, that's what I wanted to know," I said, not telling the truth. "Thanks, Madelyn."

While I was on my way out the door, I saw Madelyn press Marcus's picture even closer to her chest.

She's huggin' the picture!

I begin wondering if I could ever feel that way about anybody. Then, for some reason, I imagined Billy Carson's face in a frame and me hugging it.

I know Madelyn could hear me laughing just before I closed her door, but I just couldn't stop myself.

21 ✏ *Ernestine*

September 9, 1957

Dear Clovis,

Something happened today that's even more important to tell you about than the first day of school. I would tell you both things, but I don't have time right now. I have to take Jazz to Miss Hattie's because Mama's at a teacher's meeting. Oh, I forgot to tell you what happened at Miss Hattie's the last time we were there, but I'll tell you that later, too.

On my way to school this morning I ran into Wilhelmina. I was surprised to see her because she had told me she was going to start taking the bus. When I asked her why she was walking instead, she said that she got off the bus right after she got on because it was so broken down. (I don't know why she thought it had changed from last year. That bus has been awful forever.)

Anyway, right after we turned down Fayette Street, the school bus came by. But not the one Wilhelmina had got off of—it was one of the buses the white kids take to get to their school over on Douglass Avenue. And their bus was brand new. No lie, Clovis. The yellow was even shiny, like it had been waxed.

It was really peculiar, but when that shiny new school bus for the white kids slowed down at the "yield" sign, all I wanted to do was stick out my tongue. And that's what I did! When one of the kids on the bus saw me, she made a face back, and I made another one back at her. Then some other kids on the bus started making faces, even monkey-dance faces! I started wishing I could bust every tire on that bus!

But you know what Wilhelmina did after she saw one of those monkey-dance faces? She picked up a rock and threw it at that bus. The rock didn't break anything or even make a dent. But it made a real loud "THONNNG" sound when it hit the back of the bus. The bus kept on going, but I bet some of those white kids jumped when they heard that sound. I jumped myself!

I know how Wilhelmina was feeling, but I don't think she should have thrown that rock. What do you think? She said she was sick of everything that had been happening and that it wasn't fair that the white kids had their own new school bus, just like they had a school that was better than ours. Clovis, we've always figured that school was better because of the way it looks on the outside. But did you know that their school even has a swimming pool? It does, and it's under the gym. Wilhelmina told me and she said her cousin who works at the school told her. He said that when they want to go swimming, they push some buttons and the gym floor slides back.

If we pushed back the floor of the gym at Du Bois, we'd fall into a dirt hole!

When I asked Wilhelmina if she hoped all the integration stuff would make it so she could go to that school with white kids, she said it was her right to be able to go to any school she wanted to, especially a school that had more things for kids. She never did say what she wanted to do though.

Clovis, I used to think that no matter how much it <u>seemed</u> like things were changing, they really weren't all that much. Now I don't know if that's true or not. Do you know what I mean, or am I being confusing? Please try to think about it.

You know what, you have to write me back the very same minute you get this letter, because I have to know what you think. We have to figure out all this junk together. So WRITE SOON! Okay? Okay!

Love,
Ernestine

P.S. Even though I won't be telling you about things at Du Bois until my next letter, you should tell me about your new school right away. Okay? Okay!
ECH

P.P.S. You know what? I should probably marry someone whose last name begins with "O." Then my initials will spell "echo" and I can just keep going on forever. Cool? Cool!
ECH plus O

22 ✍ Amanda

September 9, 1957

Dear Diary,

This is going to be a terrific year! Our seventh-grade class is the best of the three seventh-grade rooms. We have Mr. Russell, who's also the principal, so that means there'll be lots of times when we have the room to ourselves. Jackie Dawson, who was in Mr. Russell's room last year, said they used to play spin the bottle all the time in the cloak room when Mr. Russell had to step out to take care of something in the office.

My desk is next to Alicia's and behind Edna's. The one bad thing about Mr. Russell's seating arrangement is that he put Wilhelmina Washington on the other side of me. Alicia said Wilhelmina is proof that our class is the top seventh grade since Wilhelmina's the smartest girl in school. But I know it's the top because of all the other kids we're in the room with. Like Teddy Cartwell. He does long division in his head. Also, Patsy Richmond is not in our class. If she were, we would all know that our class couldn't be the top seventh grade.

Ernestine's in my room this year, but she sits over by the windows, which is on the other side of the room from me and Alicia. I saw her staring at us once. I know she was wishing she was sitting next to Alicia instead of me.

Another terrific thing is that the dance classes aren't going to stop at all. Miss Davis is going to have them in the gym at school until they find another place to make a dance studio. Billy Carson said that all of the boys want to see how we look when we're in dance class and that having the classes in the gym will make it easy for them to find out.

Alicia said Kevin Lewis told her that Billy Carson likes me. I started to tell her I knew that already, but I didn't. I think Alicia's still upset because Rodney Coles likes Patsy Richmond, and I don't want to make her feel bad about somebody liking me.

I wish I could talk to Alicia about somebody liking my dad, but I can't. I haven't even been able to talk about that to Madelyn. Or Godmother Frankie. Only to you. But maybe that silly woman who called my dad up on the phone will fall in a deep hole and I won't ever have to talk about it. EVER!

I hear Dad's car coming into the driveway. All of us are going out to dinner together, even Mother. But, don't worry. I'm not getting my hopes up that this dinner will change anything. I know the divorce is really going to happen. We're having dinner because both Dad and Mother say it's important for us to be able to sit down together and decide things. Madelyn said it's the only thing they've agreed about for years. Both of us laughed when she said that.

Gotta go, but you and I know that A.W.R.T.W.D.F.!

Love,
ANC

Ernestine & Amanda 🖋

"HEY, AMANDA!"

"Hi, Ernestine. Where you goin'?"

"The same place you're goin'!"

"To the gym for dance class?"

"If that's where you're goin', then we're goin' to the same place."

"I thought Katy was here today. Are you sure you're supposed to be playin' for us today, Ernestine?"

"Look, Amanda, I know what I'm supposed to be doin'."

"I wasn't sayin' you didn't. All I said was—"

"I know what you said, and all I said was—"

"And I know what you said, Ernestine...Ernestine, why are you laughin'?"

"'Cause."

"'Cause what?"

"Just 'cause. That's all."

"Well, I hope you know that's not a reason."

"What's not a reason?"

"Sayin' 'because' isn't a reason."

"I didn't say 'because.' I said—"

"I know what you said, Ernestine, and I said—"

"And I know what you said, Amanda…and now *you're* laughin'!"

"So?"

"So, nothin'."

"You know somethin', Ernestine, sometimes you're really weird."

"And you think you *aren't*?"

"Not compared to you."

"Amanda, girl, you *invented* weird!"

"Well, if I did, *you* made it famous."

"Since I'm famous, you might as well hold this gym door open for me."

"Only because you're carrying so much music. What is all that anyhow?"

"Just wait. You'll see when class starts…"

The
Ernestine & Amanda
Notebook

It seems like Amanda might want to be a dancer. If she does, she's lucky to have Miss Davis for a teacher. In dance classes like the ones taught by Miss Davis, students learned the techniques and style of the great dancer and choreographer, Katherine Dunham.

Katherine Dunham wanted to be a dancer more than anything else. After she became one, she created dances especially to show the beauty and rhythms and movements of black people. She was the first artist to do this.

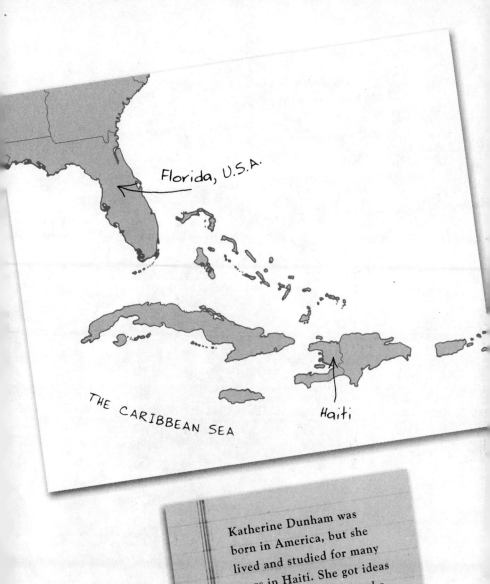

Florida, U.S.A.

THE CARIBBEAN SEA

Haiti

Katherine Dunham was born in America, but she lived and studied for many years in Haiti. She got ideas for many of the dances she created while she was in Haiti. Being there helped her see ways in which black people everywhere are connected.

Katherine Dunham was a star on stage and in the movies. And she wrote five books, a play, and several television scripts. And she earned a doctorate degree in anthropology from Northwestern University.

Wow!

Can you recognize this music?

It's the melody of the song Ernestine played and Amanda danced to. It's "There Is a Balm in Gilead," one of the many beautiful folk songs known as spirituals.

Ernestine and Amanda's school, W. E. B. Du Bois Elementary, had only black students. An elementary school closer to where Ernestine lived had only white students. That's the way things actually were in many places in America in the early 1950s: The schools were segregated.

Having separate schools meant having schools that were NOT equal.

In 1954 a group of black families in Kansas went to the Supreme Court of the United States to protest the separate and unequal schools. One of the families was named Brown, and the case became known as *Brown vs. the Board of Education of Topeka, Kansas.* The Supreme Court decided it was against the law to have separate schools for black and white children.

In some places where black kids showed that they had the right to go to the same schools white kids went to, the United States government had to send along soldiers to make sure the black kids would be safe!

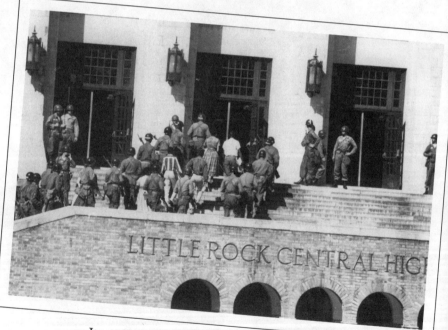

It was like that in 1957 in Little Rock, Arkansas.

Can you imagine being
taken to and from
school by soldiers?

Is this what
desegregation
will mean
in Carey?

LOOK FOR THESE OTHER
ERNESTINE & AMANDA
TITLES:

Ernestine & Amanda

•

Ernestine & Amanda:
Summer Camp, Ready or Not!

•

Ernestine & Amanda:
Members of the C.L.U.B.